Heart of Darkness

Part I

Joseph Conrad

Ark of Martyrs

An Autobiography of V

Allan deSouza

Sming Sming Books + **WOLFMAN**

Heart of Darkness

Part I

The Nellie, a cruising yawl, swung to her anchor without a flutter of the sails, and was at rest. The flood had made, the wind was nearly calm, and being bound down the river, the only thing for it was to come to and wait for the turn of the tide.

The sea-reach of the Thames stretched before us like the beginning of an interminable waterway. In the offing the sea and the sky were welded together without a joint, and in the luminous space the tanned sails of the barges drifting up with the tide seemed to stand still in red clusters of canvas sharply peaked, with gleams of varnished sprits. A haze rested on the low shores that ran out to sea in vanishing flatness. The air was dark above Gravesend, and farther back still seemed condensed into a mournful gloom, brooding motionless over the biggest, and the greatest, town on earth.

The Director of Companies was our captain and our host. We four affectionately watched his back as he stood in the bows looking to seaward. On the whole river there was nothing that looked half so nautical. He resembled a pilot, which to a seaman is trustworthiness personified. It was difficult to realize his work was not out there in the luminous estuary, but behind him, within the brooding gloom.

Ark of Martyrs

An Autobiography of V

Her belly protruding, Doll clung to the Banker, swished outer
cover of her veils across flat breasts. Her smug hand-
maid chagrined—Bosnia's Imam-banned evening gowns.
Round of figure, her sewn G-string corset sores gruesome;
new mandate order spurns altar brides.

Clergy speech oft condemns vexed clitoris, privately
sinning organ in unbiblical lingerie. Spinster's offspring
agree that desire's splendid; true pleasure slipped south
her groin, rattling her glutinous face, her grand wails from
her dirges lilting undignified, memed new trend, chilling
dread ruptures of sadness darkly streaked wish-dreams
of tarnished bliss. Her gaze melted somber poor whores that
scan route to see the ravishing actress. Despair is mark
of love, brave friend; damned heart attack, till weaned
spawn tensed in view unborn full womb, oozing swollen
exposure, her thickness crammed her tasteless gown for birth.

The Collector of Subsidies wore a caftan for a boast.
He swore, irreverently washed V's crack as V wooed Minnie
Mouse, puking, flu-fevered. On parole, Killer mellows
hustling, sat spooked, laughed low, audible. We imperiled
a climate glitch; future season is just murderous,
worse, homicide. He dozed, indolent, uncivilized; his quirk
chose hot scout-wear in a dubious seminary, smut aligned
whims with sinners choosing doom.

Between us there was, as I have already said somewhere, the bond of the sea. Besides holding our hearts together through long periods of separation, it had the effect of making us tolerant of each other's yarns—and even convictions. The Lawyer—the best of old fellows—had, because of his many years and many virtues, the only cushion on deck, and was lying on the only rug. The Accountant had brought out already a box of dominoes, and was toying architecturally with the bones. Marlow sat cross-legged right aft, leaning against the mizzen-mast. He had sunken cheeks, a yellow complexion, a straight back, an ascetic aspect, and, with his arms dropped, the palms of hands outwards, resembled an idol. The director, satisfied the anchor had good hold, made his way aft and sat down amongst us. We exchanged a few words lazily. Afterwards there was silence on board the yacht. For some reason or other we did not begin that game of dominoes. We felt meditative, and fit for nothing but placid staring. The day was ending in a serenity of still and exquisite brilliance. The water shone pacifically; the sky, without a speck, was a benign immensity of unstained light; the very mist on the Essex marshes was like a gauzy and radiant fabric, hung from the wooded rises inland, and draping the low shores in diaphanous folds. Only the gloom to the west, brooding over the upper reaches, became more sombre every minute, as if angered by the approach of the sun.

And at last, in its curved and imperceptible fall, the sun sank low, and from glowing white changed to a dull red without rays and without heat, as if about to go out suddenly, stricken to death by the touch of that gloom brooding over a crowd of men.

Wee penis, rare cause. Crass, I am all sweaty; death's unfair, embalmed off early. V tries quoting Karl Marx for pleasure to conspicuous capitulation. V had the defect of raising us Protestant to reach Mother's arms—and weaken afflictions. The Author, obsessed by stilettos, sad remorse for glitz manicures and belly tattoos—a bone infusion *au Greque*, had paused dying from E. coli bug. The Informant, mad, sought spousal trafficker cops of Quantico's brand, annoying gnarly, texturally withered crones. Marco spat, gross, fetid, tight-assed, dreaming of fenced-off prison past. Pee bag's function leaks, bordello infection, ornate lack, an aseptic ass sweat; sand genie's charms stopped Saddam's offense powers, he strangled a rival. The Collector ratified the Banker's manhood, gold trade cliché. Can't stand that clown Columbus. V arranged askew verbs hastily. Harsher words may cause violence abhorred and fraught. Poor dumb heathens, oh Mother, we're distraught, we kidnap, maim, or bomb widows. Inept Legislative, addicts for cussing out, vapid swearing. Debaters venting with the insanity of brigand deficit minions. The Author yawned terrifically; her guy, so out of step, bores a divine celebrity of untamed spite; her cherry kiss of his excess morsels would psych the swarthy Arabian cleric's humdrum polluted vices once banned, inflaming her cold sores with gelatinous molds. Lonely, the Groom too confessed soothing lower her udder features. V blames poor toddler mammary limit, panic gathered by the reproach of her Son.

Tanned, steadfast, with reserved and indefensible gall, the Son's Anglo; an ongoing spite deigned to halal bled with mouth sprays, banned pig-snout meat, vascular gout too, no doubt gluttony-driven stewed breath, diner's luncheon backroom feuding drove off deflowered femmes.

Forthwith a change came over the waters, and the serenity became less brilliant but more profound. The old river in its broad reach rested unruffled at the decline of day, after ages of good service done to the race that peopled its banks, spread out in the tranquil dignity of a waterway leading to the uttermost ends of the earth. We looked at the venerable stream not in the vivid flush of a short day that comes and departs forever, but in the august light of abiding memories. And indeed nothing is easier for a man who has, as the phrase goes, "followed the sea" with reverence and affection, that to evoke the great spirit of the past upon the lower reaches of the Thames. The tidal current runs to and fro in its unceasing service, crowded with memories of men and ships it had borne to the rest of home or to the battles of the sea. It had known and served all the men of whom the nation is proud, from Sir Francis Drake to Sir John Franklin, knights all, titled and untitled—the great knights—errant of the sea. It had borne all the ships whose names are like jewels flashing in the night of time, from the *Golden Hind* returning with her round flanks full of treasure, to be visited by the Queen's Highness and thus pass out of the gigantic tale, to the *Erebus* and *Terror*, bound on other conquests—and that never returned. It had known the ships and the men. They had sailed from Deptford, from Greenwich, from Erith—the adventurers and the settlers; kings' ships and the ships of men on 'Change; captains, admirals, the dark "interlopers" of the Eastern trade, and the commissioned "generals" of East India fleets. Hunters for gold or pursuers of fame, they all had gone out on that stream, bearing the sword, and often the torch, messengers of the might within the land, bearers of a spark from the sacred fire. What greatness had not floated on the ebb of that river into the mystery

Post-Twitter rage, shame bolster support of Manifest Destiny
renamed, resilient, outlaws' home ground. Paroled Killer
mimics fraud speech, festered un-muscled after recline
of gray, stuffed curvaceous from food, surplus fun to debase
enfeebled twits; rank debt spouting mercantile infamy
offers pauper pay, bleeding to recover gross lends from
coerced. He cooked up irreparable schemes, plot of illicit
rush to extort stray handguns, manly parts store Weber's
gutting dishonest plight of subsiding penuries. Men agreed
loving is meatier from a Bantu lass; yesterday's lows
"furloughed yearly" in severance and deception accrue
revoked rebate limits on harassed, foregone foreclosure
leeches odds and ends. Her bridal parent shuns human woe
limits, demeaning surplus clouded rich reveries of Yemen
trips V performed to oppressed of Rome for future chattels
of Turkey. Sinbad's sown absurd origins; assume the
brazen are loud, born ambitious fake to the non-ranking,
whites unbridled and entitled—the straight white errand
of deceit. V forewarned sol eclipse fused brains, arc light
duels flash, squinting as sights divine conquer old and blind;
disturbing picture: clown Yank's fuel endeavor, cruelly
disciplined by Marines' finest as grunts' brass shroud off a
satanic jail, ruler fear of class aggressor—count on Mother
complex—and yet expertly learned. V had blown
Turkish Saracens. They exhaled, some wept, scarred from
men's itch, some spared it—fur clad emperors pander
meddlers; pink slips scanned permits, foreign-exchanged;
factions, radicals, the shark "spinster gropers" stalk assistant
aides, planned extraditioned "spectacles" of these filthy elites.
Hungers of soul for producers of shame, faithful had
grown stout from extremes, scaring the horde and orphans
unscorched, ravagers often smite, whipping the damned.
Spare us from the dark quarter's flagrant Liar. Courageous
have connoted honored death of Madiba imbues the history

of an unknown earth! ... The dreams of men, the seed of commonwealths, the germs of empires.

The sun set; the dusk fell on the stream, and lights began to appear along the shore. The Chapman lighthouse, a three-legged thing erect on a mud-flat, shone strongly. Lights of ships moved in the fairway—a great stir of lights going up and going down. And farther west on the upper reaches the place of the monstrous town was still marked ominously on the sky, a brooding gloom in sunshine, a lurid glare under the stars.

"And this also," said Marlow suddenly, "has been one of the dark places of the earth."

He was the only man of us who still "followed the sea." The worst that could be said of him was that he did not represent his class. He was a seaman, but he was a wanderer, too, while most seamen lead, if one may so express it, a sedentary life. Their minds are of the stay-at-home order, and their home is always with them—the ship; and so is their country—the sea. One ship is very much like another, and the sea is always the same. In the immutability of their surroundings the foreign shores, the foreign faces, the changing immensity of life, glide past, veiled not by a sense of mystery but by a slightly disdainful ignorance; for there is nothing mysterious to a seaman unless it be the sea itself, which is the mistress of his existence and as inscrutable as Destiny. For the rest, after his hours of work, a casual stroll or a casual spree on shore suffices to unfold for him the secret of a whole continent, and generally he finds the secret not worth knowing. The yarns of seamen have a direct simplicity, the whole meaning of which lies within the shell of a cracked nut. But Marlow was not typical (if his propensity to spin yarns be excepted), of the Son's home birth! ... Vaccines from stem decreed for condom health, for sperms condemn sires.

The Son wept; the musk smell pong's extreme, land rights of man grew no nearer 'pon the poor. The Taxman's tight blouse, a twee, shredded cling-effect, dollar love shack, worn wrongly. Mighty hips grooved, glitter hair spray, ornate blur of vice, smoking club, and flowing gowns. Grandmother stressed for another fetus; the lace of her pompous gown falls frilled, arced opulently off her thigh, protruding womb in bloodline, her pubic hair covers her scars.

Grand Thief Auto, bravado utterly, extreme run slaughter spark races' monster surge.

We cause a rogue Iran's focus to chill or goad Turkey.
We cursed drab, broody Deng Xiao Ping, laws that heeded not whet dissent impasse. Imposter Peking bloody Boxer conqueror, futile ghost demons breed—in some game show confessing—a predatory wife. Rare kinds do often stray and roam borderlands, then grown, misbehave. Muslim worship anchors in prayer observancy. Fun quickie's fairly brusque, like a mother when surly; cis foreplay's to blame. Inner unsuitability of bare carousings, suburban chores, the urine traces, rampaging dementedly on wife, pride masked, failed bonfire lens of history expired nightly, mundane, mule indolence; Lord's prayer is gushing delirious for appeasement, confess it eagerly in depth: kitsch is auspicious for its persistence; Santa's illusional as empathy. No professed master empowers a worker's tactical goal, trauma's rational-free, deplore the crises who uphold Rohingya treatment or control dominant that desperately rebinds the weakest of earth growing. The sperms in semen flap an inept agility, a pearl gleaming, a rich prize sniffing the smell, odor, smacked butt. Embargo upshot's cynical (cities' growth density of millions re-infected),

and to him the meaning of an episode was not inside like a kernel but outside, enveloping the tale which brought it out only as a glow brings out a haze, in the likeness of one of these misty halos that sometimes are made visible by the spectral illumination of moonshine.

His remark did not seem at all surprising. It was just like Marlow. It was accepted in silence. No one took the trouble to grunt even; and presently he said, very slow—

"I was thinking of very old times, when the Romans first came here, nineteen hundred years ago—the other day … Light came out of this river since—you say Knights? Yes; but it is like a running blaze on a plain, like a flash of lightning in the clouds. We live in the flicker—may it last as long as the old earth keeps rolling! But darkness was here yesterday. Imagine the feelings of a commander of a fine—what d'ye call 'em?—trireme in the Mediterranean, ordered suddenly to the north; run overland across the Gauls in a hurry; put in charge of one of these craft the legionaries—a wonderful lot of handy men they must have been, too—used to build, apparently by the hundred, in a month or two, if we may believe what we read. Imagine him here—the very end of the world, a sea the colour of lead, a sky the colour of smoke, a kind of ship about as rigid as a Concertina—and going up this river with stores, or orders, or what you like. Sand-banks, marshes, forests, savages—precious little to eat fit for a civilized man, nothing but Thames water to drink. No Falernian wine here, no going ashore. Here and there a military camp lost in a wilderness, like a needle in a bundle of hay—cold, fog, tempests, disease, exile, and death—death skulking in the air, in the water, in the bush. They must have been dying rank tubing excreting, sodden belly load grows ossified while maternal guts subside; developing entrail itch—sordid bout—trophy actor show preens outer gay's inner crisis wanton unease, pixie rainbows plait sublimes a shade beautiful, buy commercial communication of tune time.

Disney Park hid SWAT theme of mall uprising. Lit, combust while cargo ship flaws inspected with violence. No gun, looters muddle through hunt season; allegedly V fled Manilow—

"My convincing (cough) manifold rhymes, where the Chosen cursed Cain's fear, lightning thundered, fierce below—I'd rather pray … Fright, shame, pout from belligerence—bouquet brides? Best smut ditties strike a punning phrase in the brain, spike a brash rewriting of pronouns." V grieves, drinks her liquor—sated fast, her song has ribald mirth, beats moping! Butt hardness was queer cabaret. Is fashion a fleeting offer, a brander of design? Cochlear problem? Livestream Twitter? Ethnic and alien, bordered colony, future fraught; come Yoda, man the Force, spur Maul's killer worry, shoot Sith Malgus. Gum disease grafts a lesion's caries, a bountiful clot of antigen may crust lab tissue—bruised, distilled repentantly, cider drunkard's liquor funk of brew; in dismay we grieve godly creed. It's passion we fear—a fairy friend for a girl, mercy for squalor ahead implies her lover's a joke; a blind cupid has stout and frigid mass per ballerina hands, crowing bupkis figure deplores "foreigners all taught to bribe." Land grabs versus tourists' lavishness—endless civil conceits restore illegalized, annulling gut-cleansed lawyers' rubric. "Flow ovarian whine dear?" Consoling rapport. Wear and tear, a sanitary cramp knotting an elder lass, diaper fecal with a fungal bouquet—hotdog, dentist's unease, hostile bad breath—exulting in affair with the Author, drinker, douche. Famous has-been prying like flies here. Oh, yes—he did it. Did it very well, too, no doubt, and without thinking much about it either, except afterwards to brag of what he had gone through in his time, perhaps. They were men enough to face the darkness. And perhaps he was cheered by keeping his eye on a chance of promotion to the fleet at Ravenna by and by, if he had good friends in Rome and survived the awful climate. Or think of a decent young citizen in a toga—perhaps too much dice, you know—coming out here in the train of some prefect, or tax-gatherer, or trader even, to mend his fortunes. Land in a swamp, march through the woods, and in some inland post feel the savagery, the utter savagery, had closed round him—all that mysterious life of the wilderness that stirs in the forest, in the jungles, in the hearts of wild men. There's no initiation either into such mysteries. He has to live in the midst of the incomprehensible, which is also detestable. And it has a fascination, too, that goes to work upon him. The fascination of the abomination—you know, imagine the growing regrets, the longing to escape, the powerless disgust, the surrender, the hate."

He paused.

"Mind," he began again, lifting one arm from the elbow, the palm of the hand outwards, so that, with his legs folded before him, he had the pose of a Buddha preaching in European clothes and without a lotus-flower—"Mind, none of us would feel exactly like this. What saves us is efficiency—the devotion to efficiency. But these chaps were not much account, really. They were no colonists; their administration was merely a squeeze, and nothing more, I suspect. They were conquerors, and for that you want only brute force—nothing to boast of, when you have it, since your strength is just an accident

dyke spies fear. No dress permitted. Frigidairy smell, tuna,
trout, candied sprout chicken lunch; devout believer expects
pastor words to drag ungodly and undo his divine
prolapse. Play Rachmaninoff to grace the martyrs. Damn
the facts, zeros jeered, believing this lie for advance,
for emotions skew elite, a dilemma high and dry; shifty
bad mood trends at home had revived a law inviolate.
More shrinks offer treatment: glum hippie, Zen inner yoga—
relapse to touch guys below—drugging frontier triggers
brain, problem defect for axe batterer, no greater reason
to end distortions. Planting a bomb, charge blew
the fuse, handling gun in hand, most real imaginary, a
bunker cemetery exposed howling, soul-trapped, delirious
wife falters, villainous cat purrs in subconscious, anti-
fungals blister scarred, botched hymen. Wherefore
discrimination featuring too much liberties? We can forgive,
defer trysts, conjure infinitesimal riches oh so delectable.
Frantic mass assimilation—new Guangzhou's too ergonomic.
The agitation for decolonization—coup, growing faction,
forgoing big debts, the bombings few evade, the cowardice
distrust spur the end of the State.

Applause.

"Signed" treaty, plan campaign fixing gun harm, bomb the
ghetto, napalm all the tanned cowards—*go back*—with
inbreds goaded, imploring, we raid Castro's pauper Cuba
screeching in your opium throes, brandish counter POTUS
power—signed, gun bogus repeal is aptly reckless. God,
slaves, bosses, delinquency—the corrosion of civility.
Money's traps were soft touch renowned, yearly. Taser
poor moralists; prayer indoctrination laws clearly a tease,
bland crushing bore side effects. Favor prosperous in
combat to flaunt cronies, shoot first—ducking disposed off,
ensue panic, limbs sore, nth disgust, inhabitants

arising from the weakness of others. They grabbed what they could get for the sake of what was to be got. It was just robbery with violence, aggravated murder on a great scale, and men going at it blind—as is very proper for those who tackle a darkness. The conquest of the earth, which mostly means the taking it away from those who have a different complexion or slightly flatter noses than ourselves, is not a pretty thing when you look into it too much. What redeems it is the idea only. An idea at the back of it; not a sentimental pretence but an idea; and an unselfish belief in the idea—something you can set up, and bow down before, and offer a sacrifice to …"

He broke off. Flames glided in the river, small green flames, red flames, white flames, pursuing, overtaking, joining, crossing each other—then separating slowly or hastily. The traffic of the great city went on in the deepening night upon the sleepless river. We looked on, waiting patiently—there was nothing else to do till the end of the flood; but it was only after a long silence, when he said, in a hesitating voice, "I suppose you fellows remember I did once turn fresh-water sailor for a bit," that we knew we were fated, before the ebb began to run, to hear about one of Marlow's inconclusive experiences.

"I don't want to bother you much with what happened to me personally," he began, showing in this remark the weakness of many tellers of tales who seem so often unaware of what their audience would like best to hear; "yet to understand the effect of it on me you ought to know how I got out there, what I saw, how I went up that river to the place where I first met the poor chap. It was the farthest point of navigation and the culminating point of my experience.

despising softer sweetness of mothers. Flayed, stabbed, shot;
spray crude threats for a bake-off, pot wars newly fought.
Eros, lust, poverty, pitched riots, agitated fervor conjures
hate mail, admen trolling addicts primed—glasses,
Harry Potter—verbose to babble regardless. The concept of
rebirth switch, grossly seems remaking shit replay, opposed
to karma—ignorant conception—for life's disaster doses
span Tao cells, improper hippie fling, men who group intuit
'n touch. Ought regimes quit? Is North Korea phony?
Can the Shia have a knack for it? Dollar's fundamental
defense: button prime fear; phantom embellished deceit
by the idiot Bumpkin who can sell out a cow, frown,
guffaw, then slaughter, end civil rights, too …

Revoke law: planes guided by Kissinger. Balding brains,
head games, night maims, subduing, Watergate ongoing,
House impeach bluster, men delegating Comey loquaciously.
Her Sapphic altar sprayed kitty-scent urine, her Eden-
delight rubbed on her sweetness trigger. Seduction, mating
blatantly—Brer fox hunting yelps grew to fill ascent of her
rut; puppet paws, slowly, faster, prolonged climax, frenzy led,
whisper vacillating noise, "Iago's Othello's avenger." Hybrid
tongues spurn French-quarter flavored scholar Brit.
Katmandu's devastated; restore the EpiPen coupon; who
cheers aloud gun embargos with collusive, deadly pretenses?

iPhone spawned two other view-touch tricks.dot.hegemony
melancholy, seedy man knows in Gypsy Lee's heart the
bleakness of wealthy dwellers of jails view dream of caution,
fun despair, scoffed thoughts/prayers godliness could spike
stressful fear; threat to wonderland to neglect profit money,
too fraught, too low. "Wow, dry rot drought scare, hot
Mysore." Mao ferments combat fever to embrace Shanghai,
nursed Tet, a war trap. Imposter-paranoid colonization
spanned the fourth estate enjoined to spy obedience.

It seemed somehow to throw a kind of light on everything about me—and into my thoughts. It was sombre enough, too—and pitiful—not extraordinary in any way—not very clear either. No, not very clear. And yet it seemed to throw a kind of light.

"I had then, as you remember, just returned to London after a lot of Indian Ocean, Pacific, China Seas—a regular dose of the East—six years or so, and I was loafing about, hindering you fellows in your work and invading your homes, just as though I had got a heavenly mission to civilize you. It was very fine for a time, but after a bit I did get tired of resting. Then I began to look for a ship—I should think the hardest work on earth. But the ships wouldn't even look at me. And I got tired of that game, too.

"Now when I was a little chap I had a passion for maps. I would look for hours at South America, or Africa, or Australia, and lose myself in all the glories of exploration. At that time there were many blank spaces on the earth, and when I saw one that looked particularly inviting on a map (but they all look that) I would put my finger on it and say, 'When I grow up I will go there.' The North Pole was one of these places, I remember. Well, I haven't been there yet, and shall not try now. The glamour's off. Other places were scattered about the Equator, and in every sort of latitude all over the two hemispheres. I have been in some of them, and … well, we won't talk about that. But there was one yet—the biggest, the most blank, so to speak—that I had a hankering after.

"True, by this time it was not a blank space any more. It had got filled since my boyhood with rivers and lakes and names. It had ceased to be a blank space of

It's reamed numb now below, unlined in spite of leathery skin aroused, enhancing new dry spots. In-Laws conquer and bluff, demand mini-rule—sought hereditary kin fiancé's *au pair*, premier breeder. No John Kerry here. Sam Beckett gleaned to show a rhymed insight.

Tired men ensue surrender; unconfirmed conundrum, bastard Assad's a Syrian shogun; Hassidic Lebanese spur predator crows of deceased—lips, ears, torso, when Cairo's foaming at mouth, splintering coup demos in torn burqas, inflating war zones crushed, although slime's crackpot, supremacy-driven to Christianize Jews. Hitler's scary swine, a war crime. Al-Aqsa's legit, *masjid* required protecting. Deny Iran nuclear technique; childhood spinster's stardust virgin birth. Gunners' Swift movement treason shook badly. Deny conspired combat claims few.

Sloughing my monster middle flab, my flapper fashion collapsed. My mood took core powers to shout, "I'm Erica, or I'm Freda, or Aurelia," enthusiastic former stories of exploitation. Maggot slimes pressure friendly camp races to convert, and then ignore some that cooked, articulately inciting dollar trap (hut may fall through crack); haiku'd root malingers, vomits ends play, "*Pendejo* nuts, guy dildo's square." Resort goal was nominees' base's nightly pleasure. Sell-by pageant queen's hair net, Inshallah. Al Qaeda grandmas half-cover faces, embattled all-power dictator dangling penury court of platitude, controllers accrue racketeers. Iraq bleeding stunned, condemned land … hell, we don't mock a drowned rat. Scud air wars, gun threat—the sickest, utmost crank, curfew peak—scrap Iraq, a cankering rupture.

New crisis climate cause hotter, dank phase, sweaty pore. Heat has congealed, milks are soy, nudist shivers fanned aches and shames. Id unleashed, you feel an embrace of delightful mystery—a white patch for a boy to dream gloriously over. It had become a place of darkness. But there was in it one river especially, a mighty big river, that you could see on the map, resembling an immense snake uncoiled, with its head in the sea, its body at rest curving afar over a vast country, and its tail lost in the depths of the land. And as I looked at the map of it in a shop-window, it fascinated me as a snake would a bird—a silly little bird. Then I remembered there was a big concern, a Company for trade on that river. Dash it all! I thought to myself, they can't trade without using some kind of craft on that lot of fresh water—steamboats! Why shouldn't I try to get charge of one? I went on along Fleet Street, but could not shake off the idea. The snake had charmed me.

"You understand it was a Continental concern, that Trading society; but I have a lot of relations living on the Continent, because it's cheap and not so nasty as it looks, they say.

"I am sorry to own I began to worry them. This was already a fresh departure for me. I was not used to get things that way, you know. I always went my own road and on my own legs where I had a mind to go. I wouldn't have believed it of myself; but, then—you see—I felt somehow I must get there by hook or by crook. So I worried them. The men said 'My dear fellow,' and did nothing. Then—would you believe it?—I tried the women. I, Charlie Marlow, set the women to work—to get a job. Heavens! Well, you see, the notion drove me. I had an aunt, a dear enthusiastic soul. She wrote: 'It will be delightful. I am ready to do anything, anything for you. It is a glorious idea. I know the wife of a very high unbridled liberty—a tight snatch sore, a goy who memes curiously slower. Meatheads succumb to taste for martyrs. Cut because clinic done scissor vasectomy, unsightly pig-figure tattoo, juicy contoured gap, dispelling impotence ache, unsoiled snippets, dread amputee. Wrist floppy-flat, flesh-curdling cigar, odor of brass monkey, savaged male crossing the sex of unmanned. Anxious eyes drooped, satyr scabrous slit, glitter top bimbo, tit-activated fears, a fake dude—absurd, a willy disappeared. Semi-surrendered; hair coiffure wig, blonde perm abundantly arrayed for fat figures. Vaginal! Distraught with my health, masturbate with mouth-bruising gum, cyber-graft compact clot of "flesh slaughter"—in quotes! Vicodin supplies to recharge often. I dreamt of Saigon sweetmeat, gut food rot ache of diarrhea. A phage alarmed me.

Jews' wonderland that bars Palestinian return, translating faux-piety; bucked hijab and fought off invasions, building border settlements; tweak laws, pipsqueak sand lot as rusty as meat hooks convey.

Dry and spotty, full-blown. Spicy bamboo curry: phlegm. Zits cause a sweatier, messy torture, gory. Eyeballs confused by wrestling Sensei's judo. IRAs spent, high loan owed, ransom by boneheads swear price tag declined escrow. My crooked staff deceived, ripped off my wealth; carte menu glee, I ate Kung Pao, my cutlet share, "fry cook or I puke." Doe-eyed harridan's demented. "I hear echo," frantic shushing. "When sued, who receives writ?"—I cried, forgiven. "Try Mardi Gras show, debt tuition's berserk—roulette for snobs. Questions?" Smells juicy, her colon probed me. Abandon scant, austere, ecclesiastic goals. "Emote: if guilty, be spiteful. My lamb, belly of poo, breastfeeding baby? Sing for ewe?" Pity's injurious as fear. Bipolar life, Author's wary why personage in the Administration, and also a man who has lots of influence with,' etc., etc. She was determined to make no end of fuss to get me appointed skipper of a river steamboat, if such was my fancy.

"I got my appointment—of course; and I got it very quick. It appears the Company had received news that one of their captains had been killed in a scuffle with the natives. This was my chance, and it made me the more anxious to go. It was only months and months afterwards, when I made the attempt to recover what was left of the body, that I heard the original quarrel arose from a misunderstanding about some hens. Yes, two black hens. Fresleven—that was the fellow's name, a Dane—thought himself wronged somehow in the bargain, so he went ashore and started to hammer the chief of the village with a stick. Oh, it didn't surprise me in the least to hear this, and at the same time to be told that Fresleven was the gentlest, quietest creature that ever walked on two legs. No doubt he was; but he had been a couple of years already out there engaged in the noble cause, you know, and he probably felt the need at last of asserting his self-respect in some way. Therefore he whacked the old nigger mercilessly, while a big crowd of his people watched him, thunderstruck, till some man—I was told the chief's son—in desperation at hearing the old chap yell, made a tentative jab with a spear at the white man—and of course it went quite easy between the shoulder-blades. Then the whole population cleared into the forest, expecting all kinds of calamities to happen, while, on the other hand, the steamer Fresleven commanded left also in a bad panic, in charge of the engineer, I believe. Afterwards nobody seemed to trouble much about Fresleven's remains, till I got worsen waging commercialization, banal homonyms to mass plots of impudent twits, jet set stars in Lycra. V once occasioned to slake so cankerous a medley of painted strippers with edema; deep throaty suck on my candy.

I sought side employment from courts; man, my wallet's fairly thick. In arrears for custody, Dad's aggrieved views splat some hot air chaplain's caffeine spilled, winners hustle Twitter plaintives. Swiss love finance—granted, they'd be a bore, fractious, pseudo. Indoors, lonely hunk's man trunks, amorous friend's a maiden unkempt—undercover pot laws, theft was her hobby. Black-tie nerd, a political moral imposed on the Swiss blunder, banking bailout amends. Eschew quack trends. Recession—crack war's a wacko's game, insane—thwarting stealth-bombed slums, now cinder, carbon; no dissent uproar, scam-artist knew hacker, a thief of one's image is a prick. No forbidden disguise, minister priests who leer, kiss, and act ashamed, slime; newly bold rat, the Felon paws a sexist, nihilist preacher, rat never swapped in group sex. So Saudi law's nutty, banking's a bubble, emirs of Getty flout prayer, rampaging Chernobyl flaws aglow, angry policies dealt to heed the blast for averting ill-health defect disarray. Blair's war redacts a bold leaker terminally, smiler pig's proud of illegal dodging, run amok. Mission plan— rivals' bold encryption—annihilation and fearing untold shrapnel—swayed us enter Iraq, persevere Qatar flight plan—random force, he bent signed treaty, deceived by oil debates. Men extol occupation, cheered anew the czarist, neglecting war crimes and casualties for cannon, vile; *und der Vaterland*, the Weimar expansion demanded theft, outgrown eastern Germanic, old guard prospers financiers Viennese. Dance of swords of Saudi streamed rebuttal, judged buyout the Felon's campaigns, GIs fought out and stepped into his shoes. I couldn't let it rest, though; but when an opportunity offered at last to meet my predecessor, the grass growing through his ribs was tall enough to hide his bones. They were all there. The supernatural being had not been touched after he fell. And the village was deserted, the huts gaped black, rotting, all askew within the fallen enclosures. A calamity had come to it, sure enough. The people had vanished. Mad terror had scattered them, men, women, and children, through the bush, and they had never returned. What became of the hens I don't know either. I should think the cause of progress got them, anyhow. However, through this glorious affair I got my appointment, before I had fairly begun to hope for it.

"I flew around like mad to get ready, and before forty-eight hours I was crossing the Channel to show myself to my employers, and sign the contract. In a very few hours I arrived in a city that always makes me think of a whited sepulchre. Prejudice no doubt. I had no difficulty in finding the Company's offices. It was the biggest thing in the town, and everybody I met was full of it. They were going to run an over-sea empire, and make no end of coin by trade.

"A narrow and deserted street in deep shadow, high houses, innumerable windows with venetian blinds, a dead silence, grass sprouting between the stones, imposing carriage archways right and left, immense double doors standing ponderously ajar. I slipped through one of these cracks, went up a swept and ungarnished staircase, as arid as a desert, and opened the first door I came to. Two women, one fat and the other slim, sat on straw-bottomed chairs, knitting black wool. The slim one got up and walked straight at me—still knitting with

doubt expecting to refuse. Why movements acquiesce?
Doughnut weapon cop accusingly ordered, harassed, to beat
bi “freaky dresser;” the class-owning few, piss-rich—
appalling stuff—preside his moans. Savor despair.
A nuke collateral freezing adds obscene blast, cancers prevail.
When privilege wars inverted, Sir-Schmucks ransacked,
robbing malls, a coup—flipping for auctioned foreclosures.
Immorality’s mass conclusive, purely fluff. The Fecal has
landed. Aggressors’ haphazard plan; sham prison
rendition, bourgie Bush planned Baghdad’s desert
we stormed. Motley shame to repent, intoned Novena.
Childhood link concurs all oppressed condemned; envy now?
Whoever grew victorious, I swear, I fought unemployment;
V swore flytrap’s barely reason to mope or quit.

I knew a brown biped who left Delhi’s Chandni Chowk:
Modi’s hate powers. Try outsourcing a Tamil bureau
by stealth, sued by femme lawyers declined income tax.
Military blue trousers unified Mississippi—battle tales
vaguely stink of misguided devil cure. Nemesis cast out.
Fired show militancy if fighting the bourgeoisie’s promises.
Gitmo’s a business fling, trickled down, grand Abu Dhabi
I bet got fuel profit. Traders broking foreign diplomacy
require men fake amends for groin blockade.

The Anglo, hand inverted feet, with chic Afro arouses
constitutional gringos’ dim Ron Reagan minds, unread
tyrants crowdfunding deceive Dow Jones, opposing
marriage march, praised white unrest offends Baltimore’s
ranking, torturous Myanmar. Guy withdrew Buns of Steel
tracks, entered suspect unestablished airspace, dramatic
smasher tremor banged Oakland a worst jolt. I blame you.
Forgiven. Punjab’s pampered mothering fattens for-
gotten heirs, spitting plaque drool. Virgin’s son, born
unplanned, squawked hate madly—swill spitting wields

down-cast eyes—and only just as I began to think of getting out of her way, as you would for a somnambulist, stood still, and looked up. Her dress was as plain as an umbrella-cover, and she turned round without a word and preceded me into a waiting-room. I gave my name, and looked about. Deal table in the middle, plain chairs all round the walls, on one end a large shining map, marked with all the colours of a rainbow. There was a vast amount of red—good to see at any time, because one knows that some real work is done in there, a deuce of a lot of blue, a little green, smears of orange, and, on the East Coast, a purple patch, to show where the jolly pioneers of progress drink the jolly lager-beer. However, I wasn't going into any of these. I was going into the yellow. Dead in the centre. And the river was there—fascinating—deadly—like a snake. Ough! A door opened, a white-haired secretarial head, but wearing a compassionate expression, appeared, and a skinny forefinger beckoned me into the sanctuary. Its light was dim, and a heavy writing-desk squatted in the middle. From behind that structure came out an impression of pale plumpness in a frock-coat. The great man himself. He was five feet six, I should judge, and had his grip on the handle-end of ever so many millions. He shook hands, I fancy, murmured vaguely, was satisfied with my French. *Bon Voyage*.

"In about forty-five seconds I found myself again in the waiting-room with the compassionate secretary, who, full of desolation and sympathy, made me sign some document. I believe I undertook amongst other things not to disclose any trade secrets. Well, I am not going to.

foul, daft lies—scammed boldly, blusters feisty plan,
shooting off, sweating sour of bouquet; praise too good
for awesome 'Nam Buddhists who'd chill and hook up.
Excess causes pain gas, salmonella-butter; banshee spurned
sound with mouth allured, unconceitedly grinned through
her gaping womb. I waived my shame, and "hooked
her trout." Seal, papal, is a riddle, strained prayers' call
sound of bawls, recommend Chicag' rhyming rap,
smartish balder scholars, Chaucer, Plato. Bear claws
unclasped, a Count undead wouldn't flee blasphemy crime,
shadows enclose bat bloodmeal—worse—till dawning
terror's juice offers clot of youth, an evil scream, fears of
syringe, fangs, monster beast throat, immortal scratch;
few forswear social re-engineers all profess stinkers' body
odor fear. Chow pleasure's why constant choking miscues
semi-obese. Bylaws zoning renews a ghetto. Dreading poor
renters. Stand, deliver Foursquare fancy rating—trendy bike
escape. Tough! Postwar Poland, a plight shared, dictatorial,
Red America's contaminant aggression, a seared land.
A steamy torch singer breathlessly renews her swank cherry.
Delight froze, sickened, a fleshy, writhing pest, spotted with
a dimple. Mom declined abductor's lame, slovenly
session of male punters in catwalk mode. A date ban
with selfie pose: jive beatniks like nude fudge had Daddy's
lips ponder ample blend of nether-glow semi-minions.
Hindustani's handy—learn it daily. Laws ratified
whip revenge. *Ton fromage.*

Disavowed homicide weapons tie drowned by death in pain,
inner waking tomb splinters Confederate adversary,
brutal obliteration fanned bigotry, gravely blind, dumb,
somnolent. I perceived my blunder, lubed my tongue's
mutterings, got to depose a delayed grievance. Hell,
my damn spot's showing through.

"I began to feel slightly uneasy. You know I am not used to such ceremonies, and there was something ominous in the atmosphere. It was just as though I had been let into some conspiracy—I don't know—something not quite right; and I was glad to get out. In the outer room the two women knitted black wool feverishly. People were arriving, and the younger one was walking back and forth introducing them. The old one sat on her chair. Her flat cloth slippers were propped up on a foot-warmer, and a cat reposed on her lap. She wore a starched white affair on her head, had a wart on one cheek, and silver-rimmed spectacles hung on the tip of her nose. She glanced at me above the glasses. The swift and indifferent placidity of that look troubled me. Two youths with foolish and cheery countenances were being piloted over, and she threw at them the same quick glance of unconcerned wisdom. She seemed to know all about them and about me, too. An eerie feeling came over me. She seemed uncanny and fateful. Often far away there I thought of these two, guarding the door of Darkness, knitting black wool as for a warm pall, one introducing, introducing continuously to the unknown, the other scrutinizing the cheery and foolish faces with unconcerned old eyes. *Ave*! Old knitter of black wool. *Morituri te salutant*. Not many of those she looked at ever saw her again—not half, by a long way.

"There was yet a visit to the doctor. 'A simple formality,' assured me the secretary, with an air of taking an immense part in all my sorrows. Accordingly a young chap wearing his hat over the left eyebrow, some clerk I suppose—there must have been clerks in the business, though the house was as still as a house in a city of the dead—came from somewhere up-stairs, and led me forth. He was shabby

Whiny man, you squeal nightly and meekly. *Puto*, I have refused to touch Berlusconi; fanfares caused cunning dominance in that racketeer. Shit was thrust for show by canteen breath in gruesome shock therapy—I won't go—Sun King's contrite, bright; planned by Mossad to set doubt. Linger mouth of doom, polluting-emitted fracked fuel, deviously. We prefer surviving. End the hunger. Bomb wars shocked Iraq, and awed, since removed Hussein. Are Goldman Sachs' dollars theirs? Salman's mock scripture's slur corrupts scholars, souk mourner's desert rat disclosed bomber's map. Deplore a blast night's despair, honor dead, and abort a gun clique, ban pilfered/skimmed chemical scum, non-equipped for necrose. Finance crappy among the masses. A brigand's belligerent antipathy; mob rat Crook's thuggery. YouTube wields ghoulish and dreary circumstances serving violent exposure; flashy, true random disdain, sick trance for connoisseur children. Extreme talk show brawls allowed men tantrum shout "#MeToo." The creepy squealing blame ovary: he'd been "fun Daddy and faithful." Caution cast astray, bare guys fought, obese too, starting a war on Marxists, sipping Red Bull, Pandora dorm brawl, cunning abusing, seen more booze in promiscuously junior nuns' home, a Brother eulogizing Kashmiri and Jewish races wields unconfirmed bold lies. Oy veh! Goldfinger so lacked cool. Marie Curie, *tres élegante*. Khamenei opposed regrouped aggressor, author of pain—hot stuff, via Bombay.

S. Claus gets explicit view of monsters. "Rekindle morality, absurdly," the Adversary sniffed, aware of faking an intense fart, recalled by tacos. Awarding me a bum rap, sharing sniff-scat odor in jest—highbrow? Transferred via nose—robust as knee jerks, stink's delicious; ogre spouse roars, "Godzilla's a mouse, it's a pity lobster's red"—James, Bond's gun flare ups expand, deadly sport. Eeyore's crabby and careless, with inkstains on the sleeves of his jacket, and his cravat was large and billowy, under a chin shaped like the toe of an old boot. It was a little too early for the doctor, so I proposed a drink, and thereupon he developed a vein of joviality. As we sat over our vermouths he glorified the Company's business, and by and by I expressed casually my surprise at him not going out there. He became very cool and collected all at once. 'I am not such a fool as I look, quoth Plato to his disciples,' he said sententiously, emptied his glass with great resolution, and we rose.

"The old doctor felt my pulse, evidently thinking of something else the while. 'Good, good for there,' he mumbled, and then with a certain eagerness asked me whether I would let him measure my head. Rather surprised, I said Yes, when he produced a thing like calipers and got the dimensions back and front and every way, taking notes carefully. He was an unshaven little man in a threadbare coat like a gaberdine, with his feet in slippers, and I thought him a harmless fool. 'I always ask leave, in the interests of science, to measure the crania of those going out there,' he said. 'And when they come back, too?' I asked. 'Oh, I never see them,' he remarked; 'and, moreover, the changes take place inside, you know.' He smiled, as if at some quiet joke. 'So you are going out there. Famous. Interesting, too.' He gave me a searching glance, and made another note. 'Ever any madness in your family?' he asked, in a matter-of-fact tone. I felt very annoyed. 'Is that question in the interests of science, too?' 'It would be,' he said, without taking notice of my irritation, 'interesting for science to watch the mental changes of individuals, on the spot, but ...' 'Are you an alienist?' I interrupted. 'Every doctor should be—a little,' answered that original, imperturbably.

and hairless, lip sync brains from disease promise flatulent blitz, jaw fat was sparse, rancid doughy, gutter vermin scraped lice, ergo foreign collude. If laws acquit all, New Jersey former mobsters know I exposed some pink: a mare, a pony, camel groped a strain of bestiality. Habitat's solar structural truths, V lowly sighed, abundantly witless, asylum psych-guy professed insanity, improvised acting off-loading scout wear. V defamed every rule and objected, profit-tranced. "Why have soft touch? A ghoul has to loot Soweto, or shit in bibles," V pled seditiously, "am freed at last, heed state revolution's angry prose."

A bald Mobster knelt, repulsed, petulantly squinting, becoming less hostile. "Crude dude, no swear," V grumbled, phantom figure's curt impertinence grasped my treasure, my mood let limbs pleasure my bed. Rapture arrived, I confess, frenzy induced a string-like catheter and shot the high heavens, "whack a Rump," a messy spray, mating most merrily. V wore a carnation, evil tan with a welfare gloat, biker-swagger queen, penis meat in zippers, hand tied, sporting an armless duel. "My role-plays mask grief with resistance from clients, to pleasure arcadia of bros growing snout hair in bed." "And Bengay numbs, black, blue?" I laughed. "No, I severed pee-stem, neatly scarred; bland, no odor; contagions shake waste aside too slow." Reviled, acid as plum Diet Coke. "Kahuna growing snout hair. Tasteless, sickening goo." Behave, we were virgins once, handmaidens aren't cajoled. "Wet the smelly mattress with sore malady?" harassed thinner dancer's soft backbone. I smelt cherry steroid, "His aggression is pure ignorance of tyrants, true? His cruelty's inbred, his muck-raking quotas defy immigration, signaling more sirens to quash parental strangers for Hindi rituals, honor dot, *Jat* … *Babu*'s a cranium risk?" My skin's insulted. "Elderly Author's rudely belittled," slandered backdoor criminal interminably.

'I have a little theory which you messieurs who go out there must help me to prove. This is my share in the advantages my country shall reap from the possession of such a magnificent dependency. The mere wealth I leave to others. Pardon my questions, but you are the first Englishman coming under my observation ...' I hastened to assure him I was not in the least typical. 'If I were,' said I, 'I wouldn't be talking like this with you.' 'What you say is rather profound, and probably erroneous,' he said, with a laugh. 'Avoid irritation more than exposure to the sun. Adieu. How do you English say, eh? Good-bye. Ah! Good-bye. Adieu. In the tropics one must before everything keep calm.' ... He lifted a warning forefinger. 'Du calme, du calme. Adieu.'

"One thing more remained to do—say good-bye to my excellent aunt. I found her triumphant. I had a cup of tea—the last decent cup of tea for many days—and in a room that most soothingly looked just as you would expect a lady's drawing-room to look, we had a long quiet chat by the fireside. In the course of these confidences it became quite plain to me I had been represented to the wife of the high dignitary, and goodness knows to how many more people besides, as an exceptional and gifted creature—a piece of good fortune for the Company—a man you don't get hold of every day. Good heavens! and I was going to take charge of a two-penny-half-penny river-steamboat with a penny whistle attached! It appeared, however, I was also one of the Workers, with a capital—you know. Something like an emissary of light, something like a lower sort of apostle. There had been a lot of such rot let loose in print and talk just about that time, and the excellent woman, living right in the rush of all that humbug, got carried off her feet.

I am hospital weary: switch to brassieres, sumo-stout pair,
trussed, ready to groove. Jesus despairs sin, the sad damages
bimonthly snarl sleep walker Congressional drudge of
munificence, allegedly. Severe health aggrieves new mothers.
Martian dissection's untrue; Dahmer's worst fiendish plan
gutting plunder, abomination … A basement epicure, grim.
Guy was plotting a feast, biblical. Flick saber, Jedi.
Try prudently Tolkien's righteous niche view: dwarf soufflé,
his blather's unsound. "Anthology malodorous," we read
Twitter draft. "Enjoyed titillation, Mormon? Passover suit
a nun?" Taboo. "Now to relinquish gay play? You'd cry, Ma!
You'd cry anew. Hindi prophets … some castes deplore
breastfeeding; see Mom?" Insisted a fawning foreigner:
"Madame, madame. A screw?"

Struggling poor restrained anew—they could try Dubai's
decadent haunt. Buy trouser guy-implant, my bladder's
blubbery—surpassed infant gluttony for envy phase—can't
win; legume crap post-puberty, pooped flushed has new
brood suspect the baby's crawling-womb to droop, V backed
the wrong diet fad while the Liar lied. A divorce in its
consequences did inflame night pain cruelly. Thiamine
recommended neuter life of a Thai missionary: "bland
food, less clothes, kowtow, semi-poor equal divides," says
a contemptible, addicted Preacher—a priest of lewd
costume, poor anatomy—a scam who loaned bets sold from
Fannie Mae. Feuds, weapons! that psycho's crowing to
blame scourge on all human behalf; many kiss the
fiend's throat with antennae bristles that scratched!
Volunteered for jesters, I host calls for run-off senators in
the Capitol bureau. Stumping frightens Secretary to fight
Rumpling's cyber-donor sport for a brothel. Quarantine a
spot of crotch snot, wet juice with mint at caucused bailout
assignment, a pestilent fusion, sniffing white with
anthrax, a Mall-rat hard drug, pot varied from the street.

She talked about 'weaning those ignorant millions from their horrid ways,' till, upon my word, she made me quite uncomfortable. I ventured to hint that the Company was run for profit.

"'You forget, dear Charlie, that the labourer is worthy of his hire,' she said, brightly. It's queer how out of touch with truth women are. They live in a world of their own, and there has never been anything like it, and never can be. It is too beautiful altogether, and if they were to set it up it would go to pieces before the first sunset. Some confounded fact we men have been living contentedly with ever since the day of creation would start up and knock the whole thing over.

"After this I got embraced, told to wear flannel, be sure to write often, and so on—and I left. In the street—I don't know why—a queer feeling came to me that I was an imposter. Odd thing that I, who used to clear out for any part of the world at twenty-four hours' notice, with less thought than most men give to the crossing of a street, had a moment—I won't say of hesitation, but of startled pause, before this commonplace affair. The best way I can explain it to you is by saying that, for a second or two, I felt as though, instead of going to the centre of a continent, I were about to set off for the centre of the earth.

"I left in a French steamer, and she called in every blamed port they have out there, for, as far as I could see, the sole purpose of landing soldiers and custom-house officers. I watched the coast. Watching a coast as it slips by the ship is like thinking about an enigma. There it is before you—smiling, frowning, inviting, grand, mean, insipid, or savage, and always mute

Distraught to spout streaming prose, dissonant visions
forswear florid phrase. Still withdrawn, preferred m'Lady
bite unmentionables. My dentures' instinct: fatter
gluttony caused fun for vomit.

Do brunettes fear Barbie? Frat behavior is dirty,
raucous, dire, piss-heads nightly. Chips, beer, chow, louts
mob munchkin youth webinar. Retrieve inner mold from
earphones, compare does denture-weaned breastfeeding
bite tit, forever candy? Titties choo-chew-able, or whatever,
acrid flavor, duet C-cup includes flow-prostheses galore,
coerced sons fret. Uncompounded factory pen, calves
beginning dementedly; milk never wins, debate on lactation
should smarten and block promoting soya.

Avarice iPod misplaced, gold new pair sandals, couture
in white cotton—glam Sean John—black guy dressed.
Indiscrete—I won't comply—a freewheeling Dame
rudely spat, "Eyesores, denim Dockers." Modeling black tie,
unused to peer doubt, so many start-ups unfurled intensely
from neurosis, spitless sports fans moisten sleeves
for the flossing of the teeth, rapper poet—Beyoncé of
recitation, cutoff sparkled drawers—restores V's possum-
face despair. A breast sways like a sex train, tit or boobies?
Surveying fat for the essence of you, I swelled below;
misled for voting for agenda of the dominant, prefer
no doubt roulette for more adventure and rebirth.

I questioned the Mensch senior, cranky, balding, freshly
stained shorts, stray shaved snout hair pores, as sparse as
Djibouti dust bowl, nervous of planking posers and
buttoned-blouse shoplifters. I notched her post. Notching
her orgasmic hips ride a whip is ripe stinking without
bran enema. Chastity's back door too—guiling, clowning,
inciting gangrene, admitted for passage, anal-phase cute,

with an air of whispering, 'Come and find out.' This one was almost featureless, as if still in the making, with an aspect of monotonous grimness. The edge of a colossal jungle, so dark-green as to be almost black, fringed with white surf, ran straight, like a ruled line, far, far away along a blue sea whose glitter was blurred by a creeping mist. The sun was fierce, the land seemed to glisten and drip with steam. Here and there greyish-whitish specks showed up clustered inside the white surf, with a flag flying above them perhaps. Settlements some centuries old, and still no bigger than pinheads on the untouched expanse of their background. We pounded along, stopped, landed soldiers; went on, landed custom-house clerks to levy toll in what looked like a God-forsaken wilderness, with a tin shed and a flag-pole lost in it; landed more soldiers—to take care of the custom-house clerks, presumably. Some, I heard, got drowned in the surf; but whether they did or not, nobody seemed particularly to care. They were just flung out there, and on we went. Every day the coast looked the same, as though we had not moved; but we passed various places—trading places—with names like Gran' Bassam, Little Popo; names that seemed to belong to some sordid farce acted in front of a sinister back-cloth.

The idleness of a passenger, my isolation amongst all these men with whom I had no point of contact, the oily and languid sea, the uniform sombreness of the coast, seemed to keep me away from the truth of things, within the toil of a mournful and senseless delusion. The voice of the surf heard now and then was a positive pleasure, like the speech of a brother. It was something natural, that had its reason, that had a meaning. Now and then a boat from the shore gave one a momentary contact with reality. It was paddled by black fellows.

wiccan flair for fingering; bump and grind. Soundless, Mom's dorsal post-breeched cervix, avid skill with her gaping, vixen affect of monogamous primness. The range of her falafel Uncle, no cart-queen, has beautiful roast snacks, singed whiff, diverse ham baked, spiked of Yule wine, bazaar array, the prawns are juicy-juice, dinner has spurred Liar's eating blitz. Her Son's nauseous demands deemed nutrition had chips supreme. Queer affair, pray dish! Flight-risk Czechs strode unflustered beside polite Serbs, pilfered swag lying among their fur packs. Sentiments turn enemies cold as chill; yo, hipsters sampling meds don urban grunge sex pants for rare tracks sound. V doubted a bomb dropped rancid odors; dreamt enchanted Husband vows perks, ineffable sin got spooked, viper spawned-of-Satan stripper fest, slithered teen spread, cancer hag, old, soft, dim lit; sandpit for strokers who ache, swear off the drunken-spouse larks accusingly. One averred, gobbed downwind the Serb; butt pleasure traded for naught, socially reamed spectacularly, few stare. Major bust stung Crowdshare, a non-event. Jeopardy gamer host took the blame, a show Riyadh approved; ugly masked, querulous faces—raging racists—fish brains ripe spamalam, pickled, loco, brains vaccined to prolong gruesome, morbid farts, tactical stunt for the signature Black Bloc.
The bridal test of the Ravager: why ideations are monks' orgies, wrestling room guy pad for joint fun compact, unholy and Tantric glee; the Moonies' dorm awkwardness fosters most deemed completely astray on pursuit of whims, built-in turmoil proffers forceful, relentless seclusion. Rejoice to preserve curved Tao and Zen postures' cognitive gestures, China Beach offers summer. Indoors, Bumpkin's doggerel chat rallies' treason had crackers preening.
How insane the vote comes before slaves won a monetary contract with legality. Street wars addled by crack ghettos.

You could see from afar the white of their eyeballs glistening. They shouted, sang; their bodies streamed with perspiration; they had faces like grotesque masks—these chaps; but they had bone, muscle, a wild vitality, an intense energy of movement, that was as natural and true as the surf along their coast. They wanted no excuse for being there. They were a great comfort to look at. For a time I would feel I belonged still to a world of straightforward facts; but the feeling would not last long. Something would turn up to scare it away. Once, I remember, we came upon a man-of-war anchored off the coast. There wasn't even a shed there, and she was shelling the bush. It appears the French had one of their wars going on thereabouts. Her ensign dropped limp like a rag; the muzzles of the long six-inch guns stuck out all over the low hull; the greasy, slimy swell swung her up lazily and let her down, swaying her thin masts. In the empty immensity of earth, sky, and water, there she was, incomprehensible, firing into a continent. Pop, would go one of the six-inch guns; a small flame would dart and vanish, a little white smoke would disappear, a tiny projectile would give a feeble screech—and nothing happened. Nothing could happen. There was a touch of insanity in the proceeding, a sense of lugubrious drollery in the sight; and it was not dissipated by somebody on board assuring me earnestly there was a camp of natives—he called them enemies!—hidden out of sight somewhere.

"We gave her her letters (I heard the men in that lonely ship were dying of fever at the rate of three a day) and went on. We called at some more places with farcical names, where the merry dance of death and trade goes on in a still and earthy atmosphere as of an overheated catacomb; all along the formless coast bordered by dangerous surf,

True cruelty of a martyr, pride of prayer bibles' witnessing.
Gay power thang; prayer lobbies screamed in condem-
nation, flavored fascist-lite, protest Garvey's blacks;
Duce fad's clone double reviled morality in penitentiary
entombment, land for collateral, Bantustans deserve
a strong riposte. Abundant overuse of evening prayer.
Prey, segregate, plunder, pollute: crap. Columbine: byword
real timely, strong chills for assailed of hate-ordered acts;
mothers' healing mood broadcasts wrongs. Bumpkin's brood
churn blood, declare wit risqué. Slum's pricy renters reclaim
a corner ammo store, bankers prosper most. Where
was cohesion for Red Scare radicals quelling the ooze?
Bitter tears, the Mensch had bum-hole hair sores growing
from nether mouths. The Felon's cropped pimp-biker drag;
her muscles rock her strong hips, squinch cum's muck
frontal/lower her blowhole; the cheesy, winey smell sprung
corrupt tastefully as leather gowns, spraying fur implants.
Finger gently extremity of birth cry that augurs fleshy
maws; lingam's heretical, siring seducer Protestants.
Occlude no jocular lip-synched puns; a drawled shame
skewed jargoned Spanish, the legal rights bloke who'd
interfere, the slimy old reptile who'd thieve an evil speech—
in stumbling Latin. Robin Hood fashion. Sharecropper's
rush of profanity's trickster competing, offensive gratuitous
snobbery filters spite; panic wars originated high-tone
snobby accord's austerity, urgently; *Herr Boer's ein Kampf*
for racists—Isolde tendencies!—England's louts incite:
beware.

We favor aggressors (why Kurdistan?—in fact, holy shit),
defying faux-Caesar celebrates nausea-gray election.
Insured mansion oases' swish carnival games,
lesser Cary Grants'd serenade t'wards dawn's winter chill,
unworthy amateurs masse rotten sofa-seated astrodome;
Mao Zedong reforms exposed, ordered Thai, paperless serfs'

as if Nature herself had tried to ward off intruders; in and out of rivers, streams of death in life, whose banks were rotting into mud, whose waters, thickened into slime, invaded the contorted mangroves, that seemed to writhe at us in the extremity of an impotent despair. Nowhere did we stop long enough to get a particularized impression, but the general sense of vague and oppressive wonder grew upon me. It was like a weary pilgrimage amongst hints for nightmares.

"It was upward of thirty days before I saw the mouth of the big river. We anchored off the seat of the government. But my work would not begin till some two hundred miles farther on. So as soon as I could I made a start for a place thirty miles higher up.

"I had my passage on a little sea-going steamer. Her captain was a Swede, and knowing me for a seaman, invited me on the bridge. He was a young man, lean, fair, and morose, with lanky hair and a shuffling gait. As we left the miserable little wharf, he tossed his head contemptuously at the shore. 'Been living there?' he asked. I said, 'Yes.' 'Fine lot these government chaps—are they not?' he went on, speaking English with great precision and considerable bitterness. 'It is funny what some people will do for a few francs a month. I wonder what becomes of that kind when it goes upcountry?' I said to him I expected to see that soon. 'So-o-o!' he exclaimed. He shuffled athwart, keeping one eye ahead vigilantly. 'Don't be too sure,' he continued. 'The other day I took up a man who hanged himself on the road. He was a Swede, too.' 'Hanged himself! Why, in God's name?' I cried. He kept on looking out watchfully. 'Who knows? The sun too much for him, or the country perhaps.'

captive labor for sale applied new board's profit rulers;
with devout believers' dreams of spreading strife, Druze
camps marauding with new blood; crew's quarters sickened
mildew grime, pervaded Zyklon-coated gas stoves, esteemed
surmise malice splinters calamity-fallen innocent affair.
Phone share Disney pop song creampuff; forget the
testicular-sized aggression, shut the federal pens—a plague,
a repressive blunder: cue autopsy. Quit laws psycho
Harry, chill visage for punks, Clint's forthright stares.

Hit laws preferred by Dirty: blaze galore ignores fallout,
Walther trig-finger. He flattered opposite of McGovern's
bent. Cult suburb-hood plots within, christens new
drunkard wives, yard or lawn. Mowers, pruners, Ry Cooder
played guitar to embrace flirty messiah's club.

Unclad advantage of the fickle, freeloading Senior's
attraction throes succeed, rammed jokingly poor adhesion,
delighted V on a fridge. She wore a cheongsam, clean,
fecund, baroque, minced campy flair, panda-snuggling bait.
Fancy dressed, irresistible, gleeful Stormy flossed instead
conscientiously as a whore. "Teen sniffing lair?" she gasped,
"I'm breathless. Mein Gott!" Squeezed governess laps—
"spa day hot?" distention reeking Guinness whipped skate,
nutrition bland, one pita bagel, winter cress. "Sixties
munchy pot, dumb legal issue; no curfew, thanks a bunch."
Hedge fund the shoddy slums of maligned, Senate chose
abruptly, whites fled ruins. Guy suspected Rudy's immune.
"Bro-o-o unashamed!" V stumbled off course, leaking
tongue-tied, misled criminally. Comey's obscure ineptitude.
"Brie, butter, whey, a fruit cup, pecan chew, candies melt
a la mode. Rehabs for sweet tooth." Damned incels! Guys'
lynch mob's game denied. Flee Captain Crook, bigmouth
crotch bully. New lows? No one to judge whoring,
so the hungry pay tax.

"At last we opened a reach. A rocky cliff appeared, mounds of turned-up earth by the shore, houses on a hill, others with iron roofs, amongst a waste of excavations, or hanging to the declivity. A continuous noise of the rapids above hovered over this scene of inhabited devastation. A lot of people, mostly black and naked, moved about like ants. A jetty projected into the river. A blinding sunlight drowned all this at times in a sudden recrudescence of glare. 'There's your Company's station,' said the Swede, pointing to three wooden barrack-like structures on the rocky slope. 'I will send your things up. Four boxes did you say? So. Farewell.'

"I came upon a boiler wallowing in the grass, then found a path leading up the hill. It turned aside for the boulders, and also for an undersized railway-truck lying there on its back with its wheels in the air. One was off. The thing looked as dead as the carcass of some animal. I came upon more pieces of decaying machinery, a stack of rusty rails. To the left a clump of trees made a shady spot, where dark things seemed to stir feebly. I blinked, the path was steep. A horn tooted to the right, and I saw the black people run. A heavy and dull detonation shook the ground, a puff of smoke came out of the cliff, and that was all. No change appeared on the face of the rock. They were building a railway. The cliff was not in the way or anything; but this objectless blasting was all the work going on.

"A slight clinking behind me made me turn my head. Six black men advanced in a file, toiling up the path. They walked erect and slow, balancing small baskets full of earth on their heads, and the clink kept time with their footsteps. Black rags were wound round

That nasty: vote and impeach. Employee with a beard
sounds concerned, answered cry for war, spouses ponder pill,
mothers are scion-proofed, the Rump's unchaste admini-
stration's protracting Fuhrer affinity. Ignominious boys'
conjure masses amuck, trumpet voters dicking for a
bankrupted aberration. A mob, illegal, mostly cracker
hatred, lubed with downright angst, already rejected
its future bitter. A rhyming rewrite crowned a wit's sublime
inner sullen, omnipresent despair. Wherefore puppetry's
nation? Dead indeed, poisoned cruelty spewed in havoc—
strike clusters squander foggy hope. Lie still, fend for grim
slump. Obnoxiously New Day? Go, raise hell.

Why blame Macron? Employers clobbering middle class,
expound Descartes' meaning—all drivel. Interned to hide
from stockholders, brand all for foreign advertised, waylaid
schmuck plying wares from his sack whips ideals in despair.
Fun nose job. Learning spooked at headmaster targets of
gun radical. Cry shame Clinton's sore penis obfuscating
"our Hillary," payback for lusty males. Future theft, a junk
Chinese trader, gravy pot shares shark fins steamed;
prefer green tea. Time ticked, riffraff asleep, Exxon looted
lunar night, an eyesore, a fracked evil scum. A deadly-for-
gulls devastation, look around, the stuff of global drought,
scoff belief, ransack, forestall. Lone Ranger feared bomber
base in Iraq. Major beatings in jail "play." A stiff
mascot interplay in Abu scene; gutless abjectness, laugh-
ing trolls gaol berserk throwing scorn.

Despite shrinking benignly, "ladies" learn high tech.
Chicks back then demanding, hostile, boiling in their wrath.
Gays rocked bedecked rainbows, fashioning doll caskets,
school of mirth from square pegs' anger, pink-capped
Heimliched hirsute pecs. Hashtags fur-bound down

their loins, and the short ends behind waggled to and fro like tails. I could see every rib, the joints of their limbs were like knots in a rope; each had an iron collar on his neck, and all were connected together with a chain whose bights swung between them, rhythmically clinking. Another report from the cliff made me think suddenly of that ship of war I had seen firing into a continent. It was the same kind of ominous voice; but these men could by no stretch of imagination be called enemies. They were called criminals, and the outraged law, like the bursting shells, had come to them, an insoluble mystery from the sea. All their meagre breasts panted together, the violently dilated nostrils quivered, the eyes stared stonily uphill. They passed me within six inches, without a glance, with that complete, deathlike indifference of unhappy savages. Behind this raw matter one of the reclaimed, the product of the new forces at work, strolled despondently, carrying a rifle by its middle. He had a uniform jacket with one button off, and seeing a white man on the path, hoisted his weapon to his shoulder with alacrity. This was simple prudence, white men being so much alike at a distance that he could not tell who I might be. He was speedily reassured, and with a large, white, rascally grin, and a glance at his charge, seemed to take me into partnership in his exalted trust. After all, I also was a part of the great cause of these high and just proceedings.

"Instead of going up, I turned and descended to the left. My idea was to let that chain-gang get out of sight before I climbed the hill. You know I am not particularly tender; I've had to strike and to fend off. I've had to resist and to attack bare groins, grand export trends declined, haggled new anthracite sales. My woodsy memory filter coins lord's prayer scripture, smites pox in the Pope; beach-cabin Mayan scholar, colleague's Czech, an older neglected professor, withered brains lose nights sprung unseen REM, whimsically blinking. A brotherly snort, monster spliff, swayed V binge hungrily, scoff at rib of boar, "thai-pad" streamlining with skewer condiment. Imposter blames crimes on communist ploys; dummies then *tsewed*—typo—wretch of interrogation withholds remedies. Major-hold digitals brand a cloud-based store, cyber-merging sells, bedlam mayhem, spanning volatile liberty quandary. Bald hair speaker guests, jackets new leather, their vibrantly inflated tonsils shivered, their thighs bared openly surreal. Play fast freakish-thin Sid's Vicious, pissed out in trance, spit spat, offbeat meth-vibe deliverance coughed up crappy adages. Resigned piss-poor splatter, son of a disdained liposucked doctor; two nauseous fat jerks trolled democracy, wearying a rival by fibs, drivel. His bladder's rheumy from habit, gin-rum Stroganoff; appealing a flight ban from Monarch, moistened V's strap-on two-piece holder beat hilarity. Fish cause swim pollutants, fright when peeing shows such a ripe efflorescence that sea would not smell too divinely. Eros greedily enamored, brandished apartheid's bastardly skin, gland entranced that discharge, beamed insanely in a martyr's grip with twisted, haunted lust. Farcical why Kyoto 'cols restart from the States' flaws to lease-buy land trust bro-dealings.

V's wedlock, knowing stuff's insured and extended for her death, tried subpoena clause brunette; endgame sham threat doubts birthright restores assigned free will. Euros buy backlot Barbie, doolally gendered; strive GLAAD, new dykes ensue blends-of. Hive mad to persist and user-hack sometimes—that's only one way of resisting—without counting the exact cost, according to the demands of such sort of life as I had blundered into. I've seen the devil of violence, and the devil of greed, and the devil of hot desire; but, by all the stars! these were strong, lusty, red-eyed devils, that swayed and drove men—men, I tell you. But as I stood on this hillside, I foresaw that in the blinding sunshine of that land I would become acquainted with a flabby, pretending, weak-eyed devil of a rapacious and pitiless folly. How insidious he could be, too, I was only to find out several months later and a thousand miles farther. For a moment I stood appalled, as though by a warning. Finally I descended the hill, obliquely, towards the trees I had seen.

"I avoided a vast artificial hole somebody had been digging on the slope, the purpose of which I found it impossible to divine. It wasn't a quarry or a sandpit, anyhow. It was just a hole. It might have been connected with the philanthropic desire of giving the criminals something to do. I don't know. Then I nearly fell into a very narrow ravine, almost no more than a scar in the hillside. I discovered that a lot of imported drainage-pipes for the settlement had been tumbled in there. There wasn't one that was not broken. It was a wanton smash-up. At last I got under the trees. My purpose was to stroll into the shade for a moment; but no sooner within than it seemed to me I had stepped into the gloomy circle of some Inferno. The rapids were near, and an uninterrupted, uniform, headlong, rushing noise filled the mournful stillness of the grove, where not a breath stirred, not a leaf moved, with a mysterious sound—as though the tearing pace of the launched earth had suddenly become audible.

dumb slimes—rats grope V, gunplay copy's splitting devout, browsing a sex act's lost recording, suitor recants all cavorts from wife desired, hungered anew. Livestream a rebel in silence, random vessel of need grand-embezzled a godly friar; bulk-buy stall bazaars! Fleas prolong musty bedside revels, cat sprayed alcove's scent anti-mildew. Gut says I should not kiss till tied, psycho-bore Jack in *The Shining*, frontline for frat standby, moody bummer, wasted killer's family, ending revived rebel horror's pugnacious, lascivious posse. Wow. He's seriously spooky; new guy vows slowly provide crowd Demerol, funds trader hands accountant file's charter. Sore opponent, childhood absorbed lactose by restoring spinally supplemented Advil, discreetly coerced by Steve-my bad-King.

Why, a Freud id! A Ba'ath party cripple stole Scud copy; machine killing on remote in service of rich guy crowned, irresponsible to decline. Incumbent, a warrior, a bandit, semi-Mao. Hit mobs crushed Mosul. Spit white has-beens elected Hitler; Analytica's Liar permitting deplorables nothing taboo. Why go low? Sinai's queasy smelling sewers, scary Cairo latrines are gross, nose cordons bazaar, stinker inside. Crisis suffered scattershot of assorted Cambridge tripe, plotters' excrement—black bean—jumbled with care. Despondent pundit's cause verboten. Imposter Tongans' flash-mob. Act fast, life's short, hunger decrees buy surplus. All new soul if you upgrade your atonement; guano humor driven, Dramamined loony mired Left in ruler Sunni colonel's condom embargo. A vapid career tantrum won, filibustered truly bonehead proroguing boys willed a scornful grimness, waterboard extorter's death spurred lawyer, thief sleuthed. Bigger imperious mound: mass grows the Bering Straits of her paunched girth fed gluttony, in sum, conjugal.

"Black shapes crouched, lay, sat between the trees leaning against the trunks, clinging to the earth, half coming out, half effaced within the dim light, in all the attitudes of pain, abandonment, and despair. Another mine on the cliff went off, followed by a slight shudder of the soil under my feet. The work was going on. The work! And this was the place where some of the helpers had withdrawn to die.

"They were dying slowly—it was very clear. They were not enemies, they were not criminals, they were nothing earthly now—nothing but black shadows of disease and starvation, lying confusedly in the greenish gloom. Brought from all the recesses of the coast in all the legality of time contracts, lost in uncongenial surroundings, fed on unfamiliar food, they sickened, became inefficient, and were then allowed to crawl away and rest. These moribund shapes were free as air—and nearly as thin. I began to distinguish the gleam of the eyes under the trees. Then, glancing down, I saw a face near my hand. The black bones reclined at full length with one shoulder against the tree, and slowly the eyelids rose and the sunken eyes looked up at me, enormous and vacant, a kind of blind, white flicker in the depths of the orbs, which died out slowly. The man seemed young—almost a boy—but you know with them it's hard to tell. I found nothing else to do but to offer him one of my good Swede's ship's biscuits I had in my pocket. The fingers closed slowly on it and held—there was no other movement and no other glance. He had tied a bit of white worsted round his neck—Why? Where did he get it? Was it a badge—an ornament—a charm—a propitiatory act? Was there any idea at all connected with it? It looked startling round his black neck, this bit of white thread from beyond the seas.

Netscape browsed gay Halloween furries' screaming
events, fur drunks singing to her birth-stuff rubbing snout,
slush embraced with Tinder, inviting altar platitudes inane,
emoluments everywhere. The Mother's sign of relief,
scent of haloed sire's tight pucker of turmoil,
lover's defeat. The birther's growing scorn. Berserk!
Brand discourse replaced prayer, run-off pretenders' sad
filth spawned new lies.

Traitor, lying phony—Limbaugh's merry cheer. Savor
obscenities, player bot imbeciles, slaver cunning,
dirty cows; rutting butt-crack wackos all, "Miss, please,
I'm Caucasian," prying obtrusively on the squeamish Groom.
Hot couple for caresses of accosting Gaul, criminality
of crime attacks plotting adversarial accountings, Fed's
Antifa media feud-play weakened, reclaimed ammunition,
damned vermin abound to USA infest. Tease Nazi-
scum apes, surly, ass-reddened, clearly has-been.
Try Bhutan to relinquish regime as allies of the Burmese.
Pence, dancing clown, adores Arabia's dry land. Attack
zones assigned gag rule meant Christian voters commenced
dirty, baloney disciples froze Lambda, lumpen guys
spooked utterly, remorselessly blatant, aligned maligned,
Right bickering depressed or perturbed, rich hide gout
nobly. Urban steamed dung—a gross decoy butt—
Euro-rich men's shit's taboo smell. Ice mound gushing melts
to blue, cut to hotter Spring; cutoff childhood needs Knicks
tickets. I fed him my rocket. Fur-zippered hose, trophy
locket expelled hair balls, pro-butter lube scent, tango lover
pants. Knee pad rider Brit, oft tight skirted, found teabags—
sigh. Blessedly Brexit Boris, the catch? Extortionate
alarm, an emascula-Tory pact? Cause: May-sexy-Theresa
channeled collective cynics? Regrouped smarting, pound
hits blank check limit, old nightmared zombie on her knees.

"Near the same tree two more bundles of acute angles sat with their legs drawn up. One, with his chin propped on his knees, stared at nothing, in an intolerable and appalling manner: his brother phantom rested its forehead, as if overcome with a great weariness; and all about others were scattered in every pose of contorted collapse, as in some picture of a massacre or a pestilence. While I stood horror-struck, one of these creatures rose to his hands and knees, and went off on all-fours towards the river to drink. He lapped out of his hand, then sat up in the sunlight, crossing his shins in front of him, and after a time let his woolly head fall on his breastbone.

"I didn't want any more loitering in the shade, and I made haste towards the station. When near the buildings I met a white man, in such an unexpected elegance of get-up that in the first moment I took him for a sort of vision. I saw a high starched collar, white cuffs, a light alpaca jacket, snowy trousers, a clean necktie, and varnished boots. No hat. Hair parted, brushed, oiled, under a green-lined parasol held in a big white hand. He was amazing, and had a penholder behind his ear.

"I shook hands with this miracle, and I learned he was the Company's chief accountant, and that all the book-keeping was done at this station. He had come out for a moment, he said, 'to get a breath of fresh air.' The expression sounded wonderfully odd, with its suggestion of sedentary desk-life. I wouldn't have mentioned the fellow to you at all, only it was from his lips that I first heard the name of the man who is so indissolubly connected with the memories of that time. Moreover, I respected the fellow. Yes; I respected

Fear the saintly, shoe-store uncles with hirsute ankles,
graphic bare heads blown up. Sun City's spin blocked
honesties, spared handcuffing given dishonorable and
cajoling glamor; disaster's random, tested indoors,
Greta's being bolder, charm myths abate cheeriness; ample,
devout mothers blur, splattered in enemy flows of assorted
attacks, Vatican scriptures offer mass, vapor of benevolence.
Vile spy viewed border, stuck diocese preachers close to
Finland's signees extend caution Oslo's Accords;
Yom Kippur's rethink. V had doubt—promised land?—
end Senate's blinkered soundbites, causing twitchings in
Rump's golfing hand; master of crime bets Hezbollah
threat-calls Comey's cell phone.

Amid détente, a reconnoitering escapade damned by trade
waste promotes predation. Men fear conceding. Skynet's
a flight ban instruction, unsuspected eloquence; no let-up,
landing's the worst torment; rebooting saw airport collisions.
Eyesore standby splurged squalor, lite-grunge inflight
Nirvana racket, stoned encounters, a screen wreck, whitened
tarnished roots. *Go back*. Fainthearted crushed, soiled
plunder of mean-mind urban sprawl, wealth in a pig-like
bank. All fours debasing, a bladder-sweat odor defined
V's rear.

Why shoot lambs, sickness pitiful, when piracy laws
burden Cheney's thief consultant, gang frat crawler Bush
cheating homespun for invasion? His bedlam uproar
component misled, "forget the deaths from elsewhere."
The confession shouted tremendously flawed, mimics
projection of hereditary debt strife. Spy movement
accessioned Aleppo for blue patrol, crony restores profit
tricks, Adlai's worst feared endgame, for Reagan knew
Spiro's stinky homily infected winners' treacheries of
tax crime. Foes, ogres, I expected a demo. Gastritis tested

his collars, his vast cuffs, his brushed hair. His appearance was certainly that of a hairdresser's dummy; but in the great demoralization of the land he kept up his appearance. That's backbone. His starched collars and got-up shirt-fronts were achievements of character. He had been out nearly three years; and, later, I could not help asking him how he managed to sport such linen. He had just the faintest blush, and said modestly, 'I've been teaching one of the native women about the station. It was difficult. She had a distaste for the work.' Thus this man had verily accomplished something. And he was devoted to his books, which were in apple-pie order.

"Everything else in the station was in a muddle—heads, things, buildings. Strings of dusty niggers with splay feet arrived and departed; a stream of manufactured goods, rubbishy cottons, beads, and brass-wire sent into the depths of darkness, and in return came a precious trickle of ivory.

"I had to wait in the station for ten days—an eternity. I lived in a hut in the yard, but to be out of the chaos I would sometimes get into the accountant's office. It was built of horizontal planks, and so badly put together that, as he bent over his high desk, he was barred from neck to heels with narrow strips of sunlight. There was no need to open the big shutter to see. It was hot there, too; big flies buzzed fiendishly, and did not sting, but stabbed. I sat generally on the floor, while, of faultless appearance (and even slightly scented), perching on a high stool, he wrote. Sometimes he stood up for exercise. When a truckle-bed with a sick man (some invalid agent from upcountry) was put in there, he exhibited a gentle annoyance.

"reporters" recast justice, Fox fare. Interference
gnaws sermon's impact from on-air jesters; money-
strutting ingrate's dehumanization, Walker clan's inept
pup's incoherence. Max bank loan. Bismarcked dollars
spanned god-club, church stunts blur appeasements for
paymaster. His dad's renowned third-degree wars;
a traitor, the dude compelled blasting since Saudi damaged
and thwarts dominion. Riyadh passed a shameless bluff,
beheads monstrously, "Jasmine's preaching some alternative
reason allowed frustration. Gyn-laws imminent.
We'd rather debased all housework." Hiss husband, bad
therapy admonished trusting. Capital's promoted
coup disputes: rich swearing battle-cry ardor.

Jealousy rings bells, incurs ancient flaws, swinger couple—
beds, flings, pleadings. Rings on lusty fingers hit play,
preachified cranky hearted regime of Maggie Thatchered
prudes, uppity bottoms feed jackass Liar's sweating stupor,
sects of martyrs—ranting we learn—blame an endless
tipple of winery.

Guys masturbate with elation—organ dazed pan-perversity.
Aggrieved swinger's vanilla-hard, buck-toothy mouth cough
for pathos, a nude unwinds, letting Lutherans mount aunt's
soft bliss. Minstrel guilt of oriental angst, banjo-tacky
boot of leatherette, sassy scent odor, Ms. Burlesque, remorse
scarred Domme's sex appeals wield macho whip's wanton
bite. May gods concede devotion, forbid lovers' ennui.
V wore short hair to disguise bust, impishly fancied
cock ring, butt scabbed. I spat pleasantly "mon amour,"
wild from thoughtless endearments (unreason's nicely
splendid), burping from a Thai's drool in throat. Dumb
rhymes V cooked up to memorize. Enter ruffle-head,
whiskered Sikh tran (glum asthmatic flagrant Domme,
uncomely), Rasputin squarely elicited a mental avoidance.

'The groans of this sick person,' he said, 'distract my attention. And without that it is extremely difficult to guard against clerical errors in this climate.'

"One day he remarked, without lifting his head, 'In the interior you will no doubt meet Mr. Kurtz.' On my asking who Mr. Kurtz was, he said he was a first-class agent; and seeing my disappointment at this information, he added slowly, laying down his pen, 'He is a very remarkable person.' Further questions elicited from him that Mr. Kurtz was at present in charge of a trading-post, a very important one, in the true ivory-country, at 'the very bottom of there. Sends in as much ivory as all the others put together ...' He began to write again. The sick man was too ill to groan. The flies buzzed in a great peace.

"Suddenly there was a growing murmur of voices and a great tramping of feet. A caravan had come in. A violent babble of uncouth sounds burst out on the other side of the planks. All the carriers were speaking together, and in the midst of the uproar the lamentable voice of the chief agent was heard 'giving it up' tearfully for the twentieth time that day ... He rose slowly. 'What a frightful row,' he said. He crossed the room gently to look at the sick man, and returning, said to me, 'He does not hear.' 'What! Dead?' I asked, startled. 'No, not yet,' he answered, with great composure. Then, alluding with a toss of the head to the tumult in the station-yard, 'When one has got to make correct entries, one comes to hate those savages—hate them to the death.' He remained thoughtful for a moment. 'When you see Mr. Kurtz' he went on, 'tell him from me that everything here'—he glanced at the deck—'is very satisfactory. I don't like to write to him—with those messengers

"Hormones promise insertion if meds impact my erection." Anguished mouth bacilli's supremely intimate, Chewbacca sensed marital terrors with V's privates.

"Cum play?" V embarked with mouth kissing instead, "Finger exterior to feel grossed out, sweet Sister Skirts." Comply grasping to Sister Skirts' paws, flee deadly course of nursed SARS patient; hand squeezing plies blister ointment and humiliation, bedraggled, lonely, graying brown chicken, "We miss the heavily barbital version." Murder weapons prohibited, for gym rat Sister Skirts was apparently charged for berating goats, a heavy, abhorrent sum, hitherto bribery money, at Burberry solemn affair. Friends in classless finery sass smoker Mother's suit of pleather. Cheeky man's delight's insane. Lipstick ban was neutral for boner, nice bust with a straight crease.

Gluttony may cause engorging burger oases and primate champing of teeth. Ur-pathogen, bad plumbing. Defiant scrabble of young youth hounds cursed drought yonder gutter tide of World Banks. Border barriers spur wreaking of terror. That grifter, Miss-stalker Roy Moore, the electable choice of a peeved nation Confer'd, "hypocrite, yup," peer jury cornered Kellyanne-lyin'-Conway. We chose Dopey. Lawyer Michael's now with Feds. V swabbed her womb entry, true brunette; Kasich ran, undeserving Fed duty. "Deluxe pot gear?" "Pothead!" I gasped, garbled. "Whoa, hot sweat," V's plastered, ingrate moreover. Men colluding figure boss of the Fed for a corruption evasion charge, Red Rum hatched plot to stake Semataries, dumdums too late chose cannabis—straight men prefer meth. Teary stained plot, full of atonement. "Men use me, Sister Skirts," repent. Prawn-smelling zombie had flesh-eating fear—entranced and grotesque—cease smelly fetish jamboree. Thigh bone spiked bullfight for brisket. Gross scavengers of ours you never know who may get hold of your letter—at that Central Station.' He stared at me for a moment with his mild, bulging eyes. 'Oh, he will go far, very far,' he began again. 'He will be a somebody in the Administration before long. They, above—the Council in Europe, you know—mean him to be.'

"He turned to his work. The noise outside had ceased, and presently in going out I stopped at the door. In the steady buzz of flies the homeward-bound agent was lying finished and insensible; the other, bent over his books, was making correct entries of perfectly correct transactions; and fifty feet below the doorstep I could see the still tree-tops of the grove of death.

"Next day I left that station at last, with a caravan of sixty men, for a two-hundred-mile tramp.

"No use telling you much about that. Paths, paths, everywhere; a stamped-in network of paths spreading over the empty land, through long grass, through burnt grass, through thickets, down and up chilly ravines, up and down stony hills ablaze with heat; and a solitude, a solitude, nobody, not a hut. The population had cleared out a long time ago. Well, if a lot of mysterious niggers armed with all kinds of fearful weapons suddenly took to travelling on the road between Deal and Gravesend, catching the yokels right and left to carry heavy loads for them, I fancy every farm and cottage thereabouts would get empty very soon. Only here the dwellings were gone, too. Still I passed through several abandoned villages. There's something pathetically childish in the ruins of grass walls. Day after day, with the stamp and shuffle of sixty pair of bare feet behind me, each pair under a 60-lb. load.

or cowards together grow fumigant mold for poor beggar—madcap mental patient. V glared, catty aura—Omen kitty's wild skull disguise. No equal quota registrar, treaty ban abstain. People fear husbandry if gonad legislation we prolong. Pray for love—arousal with your Pope, pew bro's kneeling duty.

V yearned to revert. A boy scout cried "ped priest," and peasantry in growing doubt are shocked to the core. With confetti pus of lies, opponent sounds chastened, false cries illicit and confessional. A summer scent (odor fish hooks), forsaking unkempt trendies for furtively suspect infractions; grand city streets aglow, the hopeless childhood flee, the Billy Bobs often drove Corvettes.

Techs deny theft taxation amassed—whither Taliban?—a filthy, rent-overdue plundered, vile camp.

Profuse shelling, too scorched to douse flak. Ba'ath guards' deathly glare; enchanting n-words on harps, wedding overture, sentry band whose song pulsed to churned brass, tune mimics sounds of love. Philly Marines darkened brown homie SEALs; today's elites banter platitudes; an absolute comedy, lot a blood. Intoxication cohered after Godiva's show. Hell is despot of imperious Hitlers, darned sinkhole minds and nipple strap-ons sullenly cuckoo, babbling Don Quixote themed spiel and knaves penned, flashing Chernobyls smite the blest, gooseberry nematodes condemned by chance trajectory karma bondage, where devout's doom threat's tele-prayer immune. "Hold me, dear; despairing of fondue." Will die cast new terrible imagined wickedness? Prez plumbing genetically mindless Twitter doings of class wars. May judgment weigh Instagram's sad couple conflicts, beware of deadbeat resigned/impeached scaremonger, the filthy round toad.

Camp, cook, sleep, strike camp, march. Now and then a carrier dead in harness, at rest in the long grass near the path, with an empty water-gourd and his long staff lying by his side. A great silence around and above. Perhaps on some quiet night the tremor of far-off drums, sinking, swelling, a tremor vast, faint; a sound weird, appealing, suggestive, and wild—and perhaps with as profound a meaning as the sound of bells in a Christian country. Once a white man in an unbuttoned uniform, camping on the path with an armed escort of lank Zanzibaris, very hospitable and festive—not to say drunk. Was looking after the upkeep of the road, he declared. Can't say I saw any road or any upkeep, unless the body of a middle-aged negro, with a bullet-hole in the forehead, upon which I absolutely stumbled three miles farther on, may be considered as a permanent improvement. I had a white companion, too, not a bad chap, but rather too fleshy and with the exasperating habit of fainting on the hot hillsides, miles away from the least bit of shade and water. Annoying, you know, to hold your own coat like a parasol over a man's head while he is coming to. I couldn't help asking him once what he meant by coming there at all. 'To make money, of course. What do you think?' he said, scornfully. Then he got fever, and had to be carried in a hammock slung under a pole. As he weighed sixteen stone I had no end of rows with the carriers. They jibbed, ran away, sneaked off with their loads in the night—quite a mutiny. So, one evening, I made a speech in English with gestures, not one of which was lost to the sixty pairs of eyes before me, and the next morning I started the hammock off in front all right. An hour afterwards I came upon the whole concern wrecked in a bush—man, hammock, groans,

Damn crook, creep hikes bank charge. Dow anthem, unhappier wedding heartless, investing the wrong class; fear their wrath, prison-ready border-walled shanties locked up, crying die inside. Debate violence unbound, hand in glove. Collapse from plum diet Sprite, a lender of start-up funds winking, selling forever sustained; unsound jeered, revealing aggressive, reviled and relapsed, wields a gun-powder leaning, Ezra Pound novels trigger simian monkeys. Guns for rights ban quicken downtrodden, newly-born cramping in a bath; wheaten blonde, abortive, and angry Barbies—barely permissible, suggestive—hot for play, punk. Passbook disaster, a junkheap's roster code, greedy spared. Sunday's Vice scorcher: freeloader, a neo-creep harassed a mommy's honor, nickel-waged widow; typical catcall: "stripper-whore, Amazon-witch"; "I grab your pussy," Rumpled beguiled, smarter strong lady's Mom-figured ass, impertinent inducement. Guy's bladder's like prawn scallion stew, got acid flab gut, crapper's poo-gassy; banned scriptures' exacerbating gambit of tainting yonder docile bride's minds obey Mom; unleashed bishop preyed on Author. Avoiding pneumo-flu, cold sore-prone throat, biter cannibal ogles Madame's dead smile, fetus yummy, too. Contusion welt masking his dunce-pot, V sent my Honey Bear Dettol. "You faked dummy divorce? Pot? Voodoo drink?" V wed mournfully. Many brought reefer, Grandad duly married thinner stomached, young "wonderful soul." Amply paid between groans, cries, 'dad's augmented spouse seems vicarious. They stripped Fannie Mae, shrieked, scoffed despair, hopes in delight—height of lunacy. No fun feeling betrayed, besieging Gingrich niche lectures, plot unabridged; OshKoshed suitor's frisky stares at guys; unholy land annexed, mourning departed in Sabbath coffin, huddled tight. Empower raptor birds, I blame a swan, a sole bittern pecked in ambush. Klan havoc, stones, blankets, horrors. The heavy pole had skinned his poor nose. He was very anxious for me to kill somebody, but there wasn't the shadow of a carrier near. I remembered the old doctor—'It would be interesting for science to watch the mental changes of individuals, on the spot.' I felt I was becoming scientifically interesting. However, all that is to no purpose. On the fifteenth day I came in sight of the big river again, and hobbled into the Central Station. It was on a back water surrounded by scrub and forest, with a pretty border of smelly mud on one side, and on the three others enclosed by a crazy fence of rushes. A neglected gap was all the gate it had, and the first glance at the place was enough to let you see the flabby devil was running that show. White men with long staves in their hands appeared languidly from amongst the buildings, strolling up to take a look at me, and then retired out of sight somewhere. One of them, a stout, excitable chap with black moustaches, informed me with great volubility and many digressions, as soon as I told him who I was, that my steamer was at the bottom of the river. I was thunderstruck. What, how, why? Oh, it was 'all right.' The 'manager himself' was there. All quite correct. 'Everybody had behaved splendidly! splendidly!'—'you must,' he said in agitation, 'go and see the general manager at once. He is waiting!'

"I did not see the real significance of that wreck at once. I fancy I see it now, but I am not sure—not at all. Certainly the affair was too stupid—when I think of it—to be altogether natural. Still ... But at the moment it presented itself simply as a confounded nuisance. The steamer was sunk. They had started two days before in a sudden hurry up the river with the manager on board,

bandits, tortures. Fur bellied troll's sequined disco clothes.
See Claus, Merry Xmas. Poorly concealed parody dubs
prayer's constant fandango for a happier year.
Highly censored paroled Author: "If stewed, flee sickening
compliance to botch essential stages of aboriginals in
the pot." Libeled, my jaws benumbed seem silent, cynically
listening. Cow, heifer: roll fat is sumo circus.
Onanistic play, I blame my plight on the Grim Reaper,
the Rain Man Donald, intruder mental patient.
Nymphomaniac Author astounded by tongues immodest,
winter sleep disorder of tsetse blood woken wide;
Grandson's flirty mother exposed prior paisley sense
of luscious. Her dejected flab wobbles her gait, imagined a
cursed dance of embrace waltzes gruff duet. Lucifer,
heavy metal gods' stunning tableaux. Life when Viet Cong
graves' hinterlands were cleared tragically, Momma's bumps
were sibling's foaling debut, shaker shook badly, anthem
desired rout for fight unfair. Son of men, a proud,
delectable magnate, Jacq Onassis, transformed peevish
hate's volatility, Hail Mary confessions; tycoon was spy
coding through high courts, backed by Speaker laws
that verboten coffer's bigger. ICE scores run amok.
"Hog, sow, sty? Woah, hit pause on blight." Spectacular
ice shelf floes scare. "Y'all might object." Energy lobby has
depraved zealotry! zealotry!—True trust in bed is
masturbation; Polanski's a seminal blasphemer of nuns.
Penis baiting!

Orthodoxy's surreal indifference, not fact checks that
bounce. I'm angry: psyche in doubt—gut exam, procure
cortisol, fervently unaware, corkscrew crooked. Enticing
tonic—beautiful surrender. Adderall pill ... Suck at emotion,
discontented ill health sickly as unaccounted glutens.
Demeanor of drunks. Gay dad farted to haze me for dinner,
mutton curry, cup of liver chilled; The Bachelor, oh lord,

in charge of some volunteer skipper, and before they had been out three hours they tore the bottom out of her on stones, and she sank near the south bank. I asked myself what I was to do there, now my boat was lost. As a matter of fact, I had plenty to do in fishing my command out of the river. I had to set about it the very next day. That, and the repairs when I brought the pieces to the station, took some months.

"My first interview with the manager was curious. He did not ask me to sit down after my twenty-mile walk that morning. He was commonplace in complexion, in features, in manners, and in voice. He was of middle size and of ordinary build. His eyes, of the usual blue, were perhaps remarkably cold, and he certainly could make his glance fall on one as trenchant and heavy as an axe. But even at these times the rest of his person seemed to disclaim the intention. Otherwise there was only an indefinable, faint expression of his lips, something stealthy—a smile—not a smile—I remember it, but I can't explain. It was unconscious, this smile was, though just after he had said something it got intensified for an instant. It came at the end of his speeches like a seal applied on the words to make the meaning of the commonest phrase appear absolutely inscrutable. He was a common trader, from his youth up employed in these parts—nothing more. He was obeyed, yet he inspired neither love nor fear, nor even respect. He inspired uneasiness. That was it! Uneasiness. Not a definite mistrust—just uneasiness—nothing more. You have no idea how effective such a ... a ... faculty can be. He had no genius for organizing, for initiative, or for order even. That was evident in such things as the deplorable state of the station. He had no learning, and no intelligence. His position had come to him—why? Perhaps because he was never ill. He had discharged on young, common beer-sipper, manly foreplay hygiene's lousy, shower-play tortures cotton mouth of a Tom Jones; Granny drank beer, her mouth stank. Aghast by health, cough trials pursue care how dry throat spores flossed. Cracker pastor attacked diet friendly mu shu nutrition, reprimands mouth-popper slimmer. "I'm sad, fuhgettaboutit, already pressed play." Fat and furry bears' den, I sought caprice's new flirtation: toothsome hunks.

My worst dinner-do, bitter Bachelor's lascivious. Heated, got nasty, stupid clown'd rather I gently smile, mock adoring. Divorced, goblin-faced in conception, devious philand'rer spanking boys. Pinballs of swivel eyes, hands mercenarily skilled, fib lies of inscrutable hue, murder raps he artfully told, dandy fervently would shake it dance hall for fun, unpleasant, unsexy as earwax. Hunt season and enzymes attest that inversion deemed to inflame his infection. Paradise fair dawns falsely and indescribable, pained regression of misfits, grumbling wealthy—servile or hostile. Mighty pecker ripped tough guy pants' sex pain. Ignores monogamy's style flaws, robust harlotry ahead lovingly sought a specialized foreign pigment. Big name backer sends profit preachers China deal, acquired afterwards to break convening from pre-communist days, veneer resolutely immutable. Imposter bottom grader promised truth unalloyed, appeased hearts—crushing bore. He swore crusade, envy-conspired fever; Duff or beer? Collusion ineptly required a greediness. Fat profit! A seediness. Rotter's pestilent business—lust or sleaziness—can't ignore. Douchebag North Korea, wow, defective crutch, gaga strategy's handy. Jihad's egregious proselytizing, raw explicative, awful martyr reason. Chador's precedent is troubling at territorial rate of migration. Speech acts confirming narrowing petulance. Demolition led slum ruin buy. Surtax rip-offs invokes terror, still. Mismatched served three terms of three years out there. Because triumphant health in the general rout of constitutions is a kind of power in itself. When he went home on leave he rioted on a large scale—pompously. Jack ashore—with a difference—in externals only. This one could gather from his casual talk. He originated nothing, he could keep the routine going—that's all. But he was great. He was great by this little thing that it was impossible to tell what could control such a man. He never gave that secret away. Perhaps there was nothing within him. Such a suspicion made one pause—for out there there were no external checks. Once when various tropical diseases had laid low almost every 'agent' in the station, he was heard to say, 'Men who come out here should have no entrails.' He sealed the utterance with that smile of his, as though it had been a door opening into a darkness he had in his keeping. You fancied you had seen things—but the seal was on. When annoyed at meal-times by the constant quarrels of the white men about precedence, he ordered an immense round table to be made, for which a special house had to be built. This was the station's mess-room. Where he sat was the first place—the rest were nowhere. One felt this to be his unalterable conviction. He was neither civil nor uncivil. He was quiet. He allowed his 'boy'—an overfed young negro from the coast—to treat the white men, under his very eyes, with provoking insolence.

"He began to speak as soon as he saw me. I had been very long on the road. He could not wait. Had to start without me. The up-river stations had to be relieved. There had been so many delays already that he did not know who was dead and who was alive, and how they got on—and so on, and so on. He paid no attention to curled-free perms, jaunty ears, mouth hair. Divorced client and wealth win a federal clout of institutions, pre-assigned encounter is pretense. President's clones conceive disquieted spawn in charge, fail noxiously. Back for more, in Deliverance infomercials mostly. Nixon would scatter bomb peace radical flock. We discriminated grudgingly, *tout suite* guillotine's growing stressful. Bloody war's fate. Demonstrate why imbecile bling-daddy was responsible, feudal rot would condole rubberstamp. We better make scat invert obey. Earwax hair wants brushing with skin trim. Russia ambition, Ray-Gun wars go south, elsewhere thermo-infernal wrecks. Fun's hilarious, comical decreases sad hate, no small boast; treasury payment, immigration fee transferred today. "Xenophobia feuds clash woken males." Repeal the larcenous, infract vile office as cronied flag FEMA corps' token billing through a pharmacy padding his stealing. Humans need to have weanlings—cub appeal was gone. Unemployed appeal crime's high, despondent chorales of delight; then without penitents, rewarded innocence-gowned, hazel beauty paid to stitch celestial blouse, kabuki frilled. Dishwasher Asians dressed Groom, wary that sponsor's worst tailored dress was mohair. Compelled with dubious unconditional contrition, V rose eager, fickle for marital indoors riot. V avowed cis goy—a kosher-bred, glum weirdo gone unclothed—who cheat enlightened nunneries, where V lies in slow-poking indolence.

Kyrgyzstan's unique monsoon, splashy, stormy. Try caffeine, Barry Bonds—á la mode. Withstood home plate pad, you fast pitch proudly. Sir, drug revelation's sad, duly believed. Rare esteem of Barry displays, ball envy batty hid pronto to offset as new balls arrive, and now they've gotten banned—so long Rambo pawn. V made no exception for my explanations, and, playing with a stick of sealing-wax, repeated several times that the situation was 'very grave, very grave.' There were rumours that a very important station was in jeopardy, and its chief, Mr. Kurtz, was ill. Hoped it was not true. Mr. Kurtz was ... I felt weary and irritable. Hang Kurtz, I thought. I interrupted him by saying I had heard of Mr. Kurtz on the coast. 'Ah! So they talk of him down there,' he murmured to himself. Then he began again, assuring me Mr. Kurtz was the best agent he had, an exceptional man, of the greatest importance to the Company; therefore I could understand his anxiety. He was, he said, 'very, very uneasy.' Certainly he fidgeted on his chair a good deal, exclaimed, 'Ah, Mr. Kurtz!' broke the stick of sealing-wax and seemed dumbfounded by the accident. Next thing he wanted to know 'how long it would take to' ... I interrupted him again. Being hungry, you know, and kept on my feet too. I was getting savage. 'How can I tell?' I said. 'I haven't even seen the wreck yet—some months, no doubt.' All this talk seemed to me so futile. 'Some months,' he said. 'Well, let us say three months before we can make a start. Yes. That ought to do the affair.' I flung out of his hut (he lived all alone in a clay hut with a sort of verandah) muttering to myself my opinion of him. He was a chattering idiot. Afterwards I took it back when it was borne in upon me startlingly with what extreme nicety he had estimated the time requisite for the 'affair.'

"I went to work the next day, turning, so to speak, my back on that station. In that way only it seemed to me I could keep my hold on the redeeming facts of life. Still, one must look about sometimes; and then I saw this station, these guy aberrations, planned flaying with a whip and dealing whacks; he cheated federal crimes stat adjudication clause: "Barry waived hairy shave." Terror shooters shatter wary, discordant nation's toxin weaponry, planet's grief stigma hurts local. Globe enclosed hot stew. Twister skirts shores … ice melts yearly, land in a pickle. Standards, blind spot. Dying resulted, grim decaying, Iceland's fjords consist deserts, squandered most. "Bah! Go gay, gawk at Jim Brown bare," V perjured, cruising stealth. Kennedy ran campaign alluringly, kissed a nurse, falls depressed, vacant; V had a lamentable plan for a racist incumbent's future thuggery, explored by pseud's wonderland, Swiss psychiatry. Wasabi dread, "smelly belly sashimi." Sermon-preachy livid id—novice parenthood's real—explained, "charisma first! stroke the dicks of squealing blacks." Man schemed some, hounded by abandonment. Texting, V taunted to show "Dow profit could stake you …" I deconstructed Glimmer Train. Reading humbly Foucault's abjection, elite few try dissenting knowledge. "Lacan as well?" I fled. "Guy Maddin'd given queens Quebec *téte*—young hunks' blowout." Gnosis thought deemed beauty Saussure style. Rum drunks, inbred. Hell set astray freedoms if more smitten shake Descartes. Gestalt caught guru unaware. My tongue's loud (profits cut, believed lawyer clone with a pay cut quit a court of Miranda), stuttering too, libeled why suspicious mocking rewards philandering Cypriot. Captured Kurds try souk attack, Senate's forewarning suddenly thwarting remit, hot wet dream piety, Riyadh extricated a crime deficit from "germ warfare."

I dreamt of burqa sex play, virgin glow's unique, hijack of salvation. Is matrimony supreme duty? Why should creep threshold ensure demeaning acts of wife? Heal unjust school dropout gun crimes; amend price war fixation, peace men strolling aimlessly about in the sunshine of the yard. I asked myself sometimes what it all meant. They wandered here and there with their absurd long staves in their hands, like a lot of faithless pilgrims bewitched inside a rotten fence. The word 'ivory' rang in the air, was whispered, was sighed. You would think they were praying to it. A taint of imbecile rapacity blew through it all, like a whiff from some corpse. By Jove! I've never seen anything so unreal in my life. And outside, the silent wilderness surrounding this cleared speck on the earth struck me as something great and invincible, like evil or truth, waiting patiently for the passing away of this fantastic invasion.

"Oh, these months! Well, never mind. Various things happened. One evening a grass shed full of calico, cotton prints, beads, and I don't know what else, burst into a blaze so suddenly that you would have thought the earth had opened to let an avenging fire consume all that trash. I was smoking my pipe quietly by my dismantled steamer, and saw them all cutting capers in the light, with their arms lifted high, when the stout man with moustaches came tearing down to the river, a tin pail in his hand, assured me that everybody was 'behaving splendidly, splendidly,' dipped about a quart of water and tore back again. I noticed there was a hole in the bottom of his pail.

"I strolled up. There was no hurry. You see the thing had gone off like a box of matches. It had been hopeless from the very first. The flame had leaped high, driven everybody back, lighted up everything—and collapsed. The shed was already a heap of embers glowing fiercely. A nigger was being beaten near by. They said he had caused when gloating shamelessly; a loud whimper's sublime's avant-garde. I masked my wealth from crimes' sordid augment. Pay, commandeer healthcare, pit tariff-spurred con games with fare plans, wipe the blot off stateless victims we ditched despite ill-gotten rents. Averred "bribery" gangs prefer metals pilfered worldwide. Do-good shrink favors stray intuit. Complaint's political, veracity news article writer's sniff of dumb Vox. Karl Rove, however, preens self-seeking, though surreal, ill-advised. Bank downside, the client privilege confounding his weird check launder worth, grubby as Rumpling Gate's egotistical ripe sinister fruit, trading blatantly for harassing affray of Britain's Brexit evasion.

"Po-lice grunts!" Smell pepper, blind. Scariness, skin's slackened. Unreasoning of class dread, rule-on, tally-ho! Rotten stinks, weed's fanned high, stoned grow pot smells thirst with stupor craze, blow, hungrily snack food, good hash brought hors d'oeuvre, bad portent drew heaven's revenge, respire exhumed mall rat's stash. Tried consoling by Skype privately, wi-fi mishandled dreamer's banned Sodom troll, puffing vapors in delight, bitch *mesdames* vilify men, a loud bang whipped blue flashes, flame flaring brown, future sinners titillating lymph glands demurely, trajectory naughty, whores "free-basing medically, chemically," sipped a powder snort of Dollar Brand tobacco stain. Try protest their wars on stolen, forgotten of Israel.

Ice cold tub. Chekhov's so grumpy. Truly hurting bad, gonorrhea pox of rashes. Nicotine's smokeless bomb, the scary worst. Ashamedly, my stricken memory's foggy lack; blighted accessory-bling, ankle strapped. Ahead was confetti to sweep—your member's growing seriously. Atwitter foreseeing season Queer Eye. Already adored the fire in some way; be that as it may, he was screeching most horribly. I saw him, later, for several days, sitting in a bit of shade looking very sick and trying to recover himself; afterwards he arose and went out—and the wilderness without a sound took him into its bosom again. As I approached the glow from the dark I found myself at the back of two men, talking. I heard the name of Kurtz pronounced, then the words, 'take advantage of this unfortunate accident.' One of the men was the manager. I wished him a good evening. 'Did you ever see anything like it—eh? it is incredible,' he said, and walked off. The other man remained. He was a first-class agent, young, gentlemanly, a bit reserved, with a forked little beard and a hooked nose. He was stand-offish with the other agents, and they on their side said he was the manager's spy upon them. As to me, I had hardly ever spoken to him before. We got into talk, and by and by we strolled away from the hissing ruins. Then he asked me to his room, which was in the main building of the station. He struck a match, and I perceived that this young aristocrat had not only a silver-mounted dressing-case but also a whole candle all to himself. Just at that time the manager was the only man supposed to have any right to candles. Native mats covered the clay walls; a collection of spears, assegais, shields, knives was hung up in trophies. The business intrusted to this fellow was the making of bricks—so I had been informed; but there wasn't a fragment of a brick anywhere in the station, and he had been there more than a year—waiting. It seems he could not make bricks without something, I don't know what—straw maybe. Anyway, it could not be found there and as it was not likely to be sent from Europe,

messiah on Sunday begat flaccid play indoors, speaking
quotes orally. High scoring traitor for federal case quitting
in acquit charade, using every trick planned vying to
renumber his wealth: chapter verse we impose, lament
doubt—camper winter dress with drought unbound, pushing
Inuits' cushion of pain. Quasi-provoked a pogrom, a narc
spy downed by stealth spat tobacco, Cuban—shocking.
Divert the shame, perverts announced gender quirks,
"fakers damage closets," importunate abstinence. Run-off
mayhem fosters amateurs. Guys whistling a dude greeting.
Hindu devilry, Delhi Singh psychics say city's hysterical
impairments caused cough. Aflutter, Gandhi's famed
credos averred mass patience, judgmental, angry, habit
unnerved, sliver hawked spittle, smeared hand, a stooped
pose. Speedos, tanned, foppish kisser, gutter fragrance
fanned stray hot air, tried neti pots, a connoisseur's
prior contempt. Nehru inspired partly clever notion of
Guy Debord. We're docking to Auckland via Shanghai,
behold a fray of policing shootings. Men harassed
#MeToo, presumed (b)itch caused inhumane yielding
to temptation. V plucked her snatch; gadfly believed
Daddy's mother-kissed Borat had sought homelier
milf-encountered wetting-phase, butt porno parole
scandal, lol, doing twelve. Busted at crime, the Ravager
paws a bogeyman exposed to felony type-two vandals.
Racist brats smothered disabled; a convention of
queers, leather guys, Real Wives among us with posies.
Litigious adjusted brutish ghetto laws forsaking
of hicks—oh my; vaccine-deformed smut scare's rotten
entrapment for panic, Medicare's vindication; Andes'
benzene tear shows atmosphere breaking. Discreetly,
moonshot fakes tricks with cloud busting, I stoned
forgot War Baby. Semi-gay Mitt-prude-Romney downed
prayer—antacid sauce, fortnightly doody bent proctoscope;

it did not appear clear to me what he was waiting for. An act of special creation perhaps. However, they were all waiting—all the sixteen or twenty pilgrims of them—for something; and upon my word it did not seem an uncongenial occupation, from the way they took it, though the only thing that ever came to them was disease—as far as I could see. They beguiled the time by back-biting and intriguing against each other in a foolish kind of way. There was an air of plotting about that station, but nothing came of it, of course. It was as unreal as everything else—as the philanthropic pretence of the whole concern, as their talk, as their government, as their show of work. The only real feeling was a desire to get appointed to a trading-post where ivory was to be had, so that they could earn percentages. They intrigued and slandered and hated each other only on that account—but as to effectually lifting a little finger—oh, no. By heavens! there is something after all in the world allowing one man to steal a horse while another must not look at a halter. Steal a horse straight out. Very well. He has done it. Perhaps he can ride. But there is a way of looking at a halter that would provoke the most charitable of saints into a kick.

"I had no idea why he wanted to be sociable, but as we chatted in there it suddenly occurred to me the fellow was trying to get at something—in fact, pumping me. He alluded constantly to Europe, to the people I was supposed to know there—putting leading questions as to my acquaintances in the sepulchral city, and so on. His little eyes glittered like mica discs—with curiosity—though he tried to keep up a bit of superciliousness. At first I was astonished, but very soon I became awfully curious to see what he would find out from me. I couldn't possibly twisted blogosphere's smear-newsy, sloppy, muckraking bore. Enrapt celestial fixation relapse. Now measure failure invading—slaughter preteen Afghani victims, often—so touching; planned coup's wrong spy verdict rid Korean guns' nonlethal provocation; Poms' away play cricket—bowler trophy, Singh's fair-weather game; condemn wars, no peace hurrah has my Uzi. Navy filed a crime by black site infantry beating arraigned speech, buggers of a ruthless mind obey. Air wars prepare for bombing autocrat nation by shoving blame on it, in force. In wars, hastened zeal is felony with shells—master villains' rocket defense ponder Seoul's infirm has scare shock, has rare covenant, has hair grown berserk. Baloney deal-sealing closers conspire to debt exploited by replacing vote share, primary polls duly hacked, mole rat's base would serve supremacists. Braving teased, hand pampered, castrated, bleached Mother's trophy for tantamount cut—taboo intrepidly tickling her nipple bigger—oh, oh. Why, melons! Prairie hunting's pastoral encircled, avowing suntan to feel the force; Tiger Mother fusspot stoops at the altar. Real divorce, hate, doubt. Scary hell. Heinous puppet slurs Mexican side. Primaries are layoffs fueling cannon fodder, brat's brood goes broke for votes: Congressional campaigns win lunatic.

"My sad, doe-eyed dear: die." Aborted too emotional, butt sex is tacit healthcare; it's subtly absurd, too. Manifesto shows rhyming through zealot snubbing syntax publicly. We're not stupid, honestly boo. Your Pope's too medieval; byelaws proposed to forswear looting, greed recession's mass futile sustained cancers in a rebel Tajikistan, war torn. We minimize deferred strike cyber risks; stiff virtuosity fortified a milf-lover's sip of cougar deliciousness. Bratwurst rivals admonished butchery's boon; Spike Lee blamed wantonly dubious Tootsie, Hollywood's grindhouse zombie. My movement modesty imagine what I had in me to make it worth his while. It was very pretty to see how he baffled himself, for in truth my body was full only of chills, and my head had nothing in it but that wretched steamboat business! It was evident he took me for a perfectly shameless prevaricator. At last he got angry, and, to conceal a movement of furious annoyance, he yawned. I rose. Then I noticed a small sketch in oils, on a panel, representing a woman, draped and blindfolded, carrying a lighted torch. The background was sombre—almost black. The movement of the woman was stately, and the effect of the torchlight on the face was sinister.

"It arrested me, and he stood by civilly, holding an empty half-pint champagne bottle (medical comforts) with the candle stuck in it. To my question he said Mr. Kurtz had painted this—in this very station more than a year ago—while waiting for means to go to his trading post. 'Tell me, pray,' said I, 'who is this Mr. Kurtz?'

"'The chief of the Inner Station,' he answered in a short tone, looking away. 'Much obliged,' I said, laughing. 'And you are the brickmaker of the Central Station. Every one knows that.' He was silent for a while. 'He is a prodigy,' he said at last. 'He is an emissary of pity and science and progress, and devil knows what else. We want,' he began to declaim suddenly, 'for the guidance of the cause intrusted to us by Europe, so to speak, higher intelligence, wide sympathies, a singleness of purpose.' 'Who says that?' I asked. 'Lots of them,' he replied. 'Some even write that; and so he comes here, a special being, as you ought to know.' 'Why ought I to know?' I interrupted, really surprised. He paid no attention. 'Yes. Today he is chief of the best station, next year he will be assistant-manager, two years more and ... but I dare-say you know

in passion sought my frenemy do naked birth in style.
Prisons levy gritty cruelty, hourly shackled in cells foreign
youth; sky lobby caused fuel's smoky ordeals; end white bread;
sad, loving enigma, red-headed, deep-throat mistress
with malevolently groovy aura, fervently blameless
pre-married caper. A Nazi fought nasty, planned token zeal
recruitment, bi-curious flamboyance beyond Lesbos.
Shanghai lotus, eggroll wretch embroils ornamental
Orient in Confucian frame of mind, scolded Carrie Lam
incited purge. Her crackdown grows stronger—the most flak.
Inducement of confusion cause greatly planned, the arrest
roster forthright honors trace of Britisher.

"He ingested infancy's food," maliciously trolling a Lefty-
aligned campaign, Donald's (genital fungus) mister
Bannon sucking tit. New direction, V fled with a curse,
deflated, dissing mystery Asian doorman, Amir So-So—
style-baiting door queens to "tofu" piss-taking host.
"Wealthy prey, semi-new business in the works?"

Relief from discrimination, meandered with a court
loan, Brooklyn to stay. Fungicide's biped gassing. Tanned
newcomer mistaken for a mental patient. Web rerun
grows flat. Hit show's violent, more hostile, militia novelty,
pre-pederast. Elysium's ancillary committee alliance banned
concessioned comatose pot spells. Relaunch treaty ban to
defame summary order tyrants' launder laws, distrusted
hubris, lie or joke for new leak, liar embellishments, trite
litanies, a dwindled jester circus. "New expat eye mask?"
Spots of phlegm, sleepy bride. Dumb heathens fight back;
banned Rove v. … Ranciere's essential freeing value fought
Rousseau's. Guy Fawkes sky aglow? Scion's corrupted,
clearly chastised, displayed condescension. Less Kuwaiti
mischief for annexation, West fears we're filthy, a distant
scavenger who steers war land … applied hairspray, bureau

what he will be in two years' time. You are of the new gang—the gang of virtue. The same people who sent him specially also recommended you. Oh, don't say no. I've my own eyes to trust.' Light dawned upon me. My dear aunt's influential acquaintances were producing an unexpected effect upon that young man. I nearly burst into a laugh. 'Do you read the Company's confidential correspondence?' I asked. He hadn't a word to say. It was great fun. 'When Mr. Kurtz,' I continued, severely, 'is General Manager, you won't have the opportunity.'

"He blew the candle out suddenly, and we went outside. The moon had risen. Black figures strolled about listlessly, pouring water on the glow, whence proceeded a sound of hissing; steam ascended in the moonlight, the beaten nigger groaned somewhere. 'What a row the brute makes!' said the indefatigable man with the moustaches, appearing near us. 'Serve him right. Transgression—punishment—bang! Pitiless, pitiless. That's the only way. This will prevent all conflagrations for the future. I was just telling the manager …' He noticed my companion, and became crestfallen all at once. 'Not in bed yet,' he said, with a kind of servile heartiness; 'it's so natural. Ha! Danger—agitation.' He vanished. I went on to the riverside, and the other followed me. I heard a scathing murmur at my ear, 'Heap of muffs—go to.' The pilgrims could be seen in knots gesticulating, discussing. Several had still their staves in their hands. I verily believe they took these sticks to bed with them. Beyond the fence the forest stood up spectrally in the moonlight, and through that dim stir, through the faint sounds of that lamentable courtyard, the silence of the land went home to one's very heart—its mystery, its greatness, the amazing reality of its concealed life. The hurt nigger moaned feebly somewhere near by, and

plot evil being booyah's crime. Lunar rockers, Wu-Tang—
the Clan for curfew. The lame weasel who's venting zealotry:
"Puerto Rico's mended"; *puto* combed, they know. Hive
mind clone lies combust. "I want my Mommy," I fear Kant's
existential complacencies spur inducing an unelected
defect, a gauntlet-run plan. Privately skirting flu and staph,
booboo freed her gluttony's consequential obese problems.
The nasty rat-eaten, furred toupée, bit sparse, pate shone.
Rehnquist rehearsed ineptitude theory, electoral canvassers
condoned backers' dollar surety.

Abuser scandal, rout publicly president's *arbeit*.
Buffoons lack reason. Quack leaders scold aloud viciously,
falling dollar from escrow, sense conceded profound mis-
giving; dream descent in silver spoon plight, elite on Twitter
droned unfair. "Drop the cow, refute steaks!" pled a
Sindhi, amicable trans mister, blue lashes endearing, fear-
less, burning bright. Dance session—Fun-Da-Mental!
Britishers' wittiness. Raps for dhoti play. Pigswill event,
small compensations torture loser. "I distrust swear-in
spectacular ..." See POTUS try compassion, planned
inflame "pest" problem, wall affronts. Got in Fed
debt instead with maligned of hostile Party mess; Swiss
collateral. Campaigner allegation established. High tantrum,
Scooter Fibber lied, can't recover probity. Libeled debasing
further of Zaire, "Fisticuffs—no coup!" The victims
mutely grieving, shots reciprocating, incoming. General
standstill, escapes impair plans. Summarily deceived, may
Muftis' scripts skew Bethlehem. In strong defense, the
oppressed would eventually win commune rights,
damned roof rat swindlers threw sustained rounds off
reprehensible sport. Scarred, The Violence of the Lamb's
scent combs through Gumb's scary art—his misery,
his waitress, the face-razing insanity of his congealed knife.
Pervert killer sewn sweetly Mom's hair, clear dye-blend,

then fetched a deep sigh that made me mend my pace away from there. I felt a hand introducing itself under my arm. 'My dear sir,' said the fellow, 'I don't want to be misunderstood, and especially by you, who will see Mr. Kurtz long before I can have that pleasure. I wouldn't like him to get a false idea of my disposition ...'

"I let him run on, this papier-maché Mephistopheles, and it seemed to me that if I tried I could poke my forefinger through him, and would find nothing inside but a little loose dirt, maybe. He, don't you see, had been planning to be assistant-manager by and by under the present man, and I could see that the coming of that Kurtz had upset them both not a little. He talked precipitately, and I did not try to stop him. I had my shoulders against the wreck of my steamer, hauled up on the slope like a carcass of some big river animal. The smell of mud, of primeval mud, by Jove! was in my nostrils, the high stillness of primeval forest was before my eyes; there were shiny patches on the black creek. The moon had spread over everything a thin layer of silver—over the rank grass, over the mud, upon the wall of matted vegetation standing higher than the wall of a temple, over the great river I could see through a sombre gap glittering, glittering, as it flowed broadly by without a murmur. All this was great, expectant, mute, while the man jabbered about himself. I wondered whether the stillness on the face of the immensity looking at us two were meant as an appeal or as a menace. What were we who had strayed in here? Could we handle that dumb thing, or would it handle us? I felt how big, how confoundedly big, was that thing that couldn't talk, and perhaps was deaf as well. What was in there? I could see a little ivory coming out from there, and I had heard when stretched the creep's dye act gravely rends guy face obey dom wear. Stifled, unmanned in perusing his death, hunter by charm. "I prefer red stiletto." My beau monde beauty, Miss Wonder Wood, gland vasectomy adieu, you will be Sister Skirts, strongly sore hymen's shag-cat treasure. Effluent striking who spreads the gonorrhea from my piss emission.

Try getting funk on with nappy-hair sashay. Mexico cities banned bit-streamed movie chat; homicide by dude woke "Psycho Killer" crooning band; stewed rind dumpling with fried pumpernickel-juice squirt daily. Bemoaned jury, Chelsea Manning's truly a sister-traveler; tyrant's why others' unpleasant ban as why would-be hacker's busting caught backwards led unwed men's growth spots to shrivel. We gawped legitimately, end guided plot Y2 bombing. Sly grab by Soviets incensed the heck off Crimea, mauled asunder hope: cyber-Marxists or bumbling trigger radical? A well of blood, of adrenal blood—why clove?—washing my tonsils, third eye grimace of pineal prophets rose demoralized; leather Nike flashes sponsor crack freak. Khartoum had dead quota, treachery flings vermin slayer off kilter—sober repentance, soldier for blood, solemn recalls of fetid devastation; slanting wise, venerable oriental, odor of grave digger, dry wood; flee to the border, flag quivering, flickering, has bestowed oddly hybrid bouts of fervor. POTUS was State defendant; news trial began gathered upon his wealth. A drunken pleasure to witness the disgrace of serving penalty, brooking matters few assent has fan ideal for master fetish. Attorneys sue Band-Aid premier. Would-be vandal gas guzzling for crooked scandal fuss. I smelled sow, pig sow, hog-bound piggly pig, paws crackling, fat mutant hog, ham for scraps, ghost pepper smell. Hot sauce, beware! Try fruity. A griddle fiery stuffing snout, compare ham's quiet burp.

Mr. Kurtz was in there. I had heard enough about it, too—God knows! Yet somehow it didn't bring any image with it—no more than if I had been told an angel or a fiend was in there. I believed it in the same way one of you might believe there are inhabitants in the planet Mars. I knew once a Scotch sailmaker who was certain, dead sure, there were people in Mars. If you asked him for some idea how they looked and behaved, he would get shy and mutter something about 'walking on all-fours.' If you as much as smiled, he would—though a man of sixty—offer to fight you. I would not have gone so far as to fight for Kurtz, but I went for him near enough to a lie. You know I hate, detest, and can't bear a lie, not because I am straighter than the rest of us, but simply because it appalls me. There is a taint of death, a flavour of mortality in lies—which is exactly what I hate and detest in the world—what I want to forget. It makes me miserable and sick, like biting something rotten would do. Temperament, I suppose. Well, I went near enough to it by letting the young fool there believe anything he liked to imagine as to my influence in Europe. I became in an instant as much of a pretence as the rest of the bewitched pilgrims. This simply because I had a notion it somehow would be of help to that Kurtz whom at the time I did not see—you understand. He was just a word for me. I did not see the man in the name any more than you do. Do you see him? Do you see the story? Do you see anything? It seems to me I am trying to tell you a dream—making a vain attempt, because no relation of a dream can convey the dream-sensation, that commingling of absurdity, surprise, and bewilderment in a tremor of struggling revolt, that notion of being captured by the incredible which is of the very essence of dreams …"

Trigger words poison air. My absurd rebuff was shouted,
boo—sod those! Death dumb cows in Britain, immensely
priggish cricket—poor orphans stiff by gangrene, olden
painful oral-cleaned jaws despair. Guaranteed wit in
a shamed gay, run from footlights, agreed there's star
extravagance in Hispanic bars. A nuisance, a botched
jail breaker whose cause worsens, fled pure extra-legal
cigars. In newscast, grim portion Crimea, foul play, lewd
and depraved, ensured Bed-Stuy aflutter, bumbling
aloud "talking of Cold Wars." If losers' lunch is mildly
stewed—soda ban's so iffy—order two Lite Dew. Plywood
cot as lawn sofa has delight for Skirts, but Biden's boring,
merely fluff to defy. Euro debate, protest, demand,
clarify money laws; finance greater anchors West's coffers;
butt pimply with sores, shit enthralls me. Fairies purr
sainted breath, a waiver of morality in guys—richest
fled factory hot climate, planned congesting suburbs—not
detente Soviet. Innately irritable slapstick highlighting
Rump ring's wanton dude-doo. Embezzlement, Idaho's.
Relevant fear an' stuff an' shit. Digressing: Enron
fuel scare aggrieved Chevy dream unbribed, true assassin
alumni's affluence is Arab. I inflame inane infant a touch
softer sixth sense after test offers unhinged symptoms.
Sophistry deplores iPad promotion income now, foodie
for Yelp; tube aborts womb, splatter crime by autopsy—
rue motherland. Freedom's Rasta colony! Ahmad Bashir,
Sudan, in insane messy war. San, Zulu, Hutu freedom?
Subdue territory? Who knew bigamy ring? Extreme whoopee.
I'm applying T-cell cure, supreme vape in a vein, direct,
installed augmentation offers steam ban soufflé bloodstream-
dilation, splat-bomb tingling of perversity, disguise
manned free-will foments inner terror of humbling assault,
explosion foreseeing raptured, hyper-indelible witch
pissed off the merry peasants of Rheims.

He was silent for a while.

"No, it is impossible; it is impossible to convey the life-sensation of any given epoch of one's existence—that which makes its truth, its meaning—its subtle and penetrating essence. It is impossible. We live, as we dream—alone."

He paused again as if reflecting, then added:

"Of course in this you fellows see more than I could then. You see me, whom you know ..."

It had become so pitch dark that we listeners could hardly see one another. For a long time already he, sitting apart, had been no more to us than a voice. There was not a word from anybody. The others might have been asleep, but I was awake. I listened, I listened on the watch for the sentence, for the word, that would give me the clue to the faint uneasiness inspired by this narrative that seemed to shape itself without human lips in the heavy night-air of the river.

"... Yes—I let him run on," Marlow began again, "and think what he pleased about the powers that were behind me. I did! And there was nothing behind me! There was nothing but that wretched, old, mangled steamboat I was leaning against, while he talked fluently about 'the necessity for every man to get on.' 'And when one comes out here, you conceive, it is not to gaze at the moon.' Mr. Kurtz was a 'universal genius,' but even a genius would find it easier to work with 'adequate tools—intelligent men.' He did not make bricks—why, there was a physical impossibility in the way—as I was well aware; and if he did secretarial work for the manager, it was because

She was violent, not servile.

Obit's irresponsible; pity's improbable, too; obey the strife-cessation's homily driven sweet talk of Son's persistence—language breaks his tooth, his weaning—his suckled, evacuating penance. Guilt is phenomenal. Forgive and redeem our Joan.

V caused a strain, avid erecting when flaccid:

"Remorse is bliss, youth mellows discordant, my brood hen. Eulogy, womb to grow ..."

Urad besan, sonth, mirch, saag paneer, cinnamon stewed, *haldi, jeera, paan, aata. Gora*, wrong rhyme, lol, read Hindi, shitting a fart, serene, so virtuous can rejoice. Rebels fought absurd romp, belly floppy. A mother's fright was seeing a creep's gutter balls reshape. Positioned, guy stiffened on her crotch for an entrance, over-furred rat you'd quickly curfew for restraint, bum queasiness required sinus laxative scat, reamed agape it smells. We doubt Susan Smith is machete nightmare of a killer.

"... Let's try getting guns gone," bravo a ban campaign, has pink lobby ceased to flout its proudest banners divinely? Amid canned applause blushing supinely, Cher stalls, thrusting butt, perfected gold-dangled theme, rolled eyeballs queening, augments tightly locked, suitably all-out; the aesthetically poor, sensory sham, spew venom: Land then succumbs, doubt, fear, to achieve wiki's plot who praise that buffoon. Icarus sponsors "plumy thermal grievance," sub-reason malicious mood, mind inferior to spurt zilch, obstinate fool's incel resentment. Seeded pot cake licks—high, wherefore's the criminal responsibility: Pinochet pays Midol's chem warfare? Grand jury cedes dictatorial Turks ordered massacre. Ignored recourse, 'no sensible man rejects wantonly the confidence of his superiors.' Did I see it? I saw it. What more did I want? What I really wanted was rivets, by heaven! Rivets. To get on with the work—to stop the hole. Rivets I wanted. There were cases of them down at the coast—cases—piled up—burst—split! You kicked a loose rivet at every second step in that station-yard on the hillside. Rivets had rolled into the grove of death. You could fill your pockets with rivets for the trouble of stooping down—and there wasn't one rivet to be found where it was wanted. We had plates that would do, but nothing to fasten them with. And every week the messenger, a long negro, letter-bag on shoulder and staff in hand, left our station for the coast. And several times a week a coast caravan came in with trade goods—ghastly glazed calico that made you shudder only to look at it, glass beads value about a penny a quart, confounded spotted cotton handkerchiefs. And no rivets. Three carriers could have brought all that was wanted to set that steam-boat afloat.

"He was becoming confidential now, but I fancy my unresponsive attitude must have exasperated him at last, for he judged it necessary to inform me he feared neither God nor devil, let alone any mere man. I said I could see that very well, but what I wanted was a certain quantity of rivets—and rivets were what really Mr. Kurtz wanted, if he had only known it. Now letters went to the coast every week. 'My dear sir,' he cried, 'I write from dictation.' I demanded rivets. There was a way—for an intelligent man. He changed his manner; became very cold, and suddenly began to talk about a hippopotamus; wondered whether sleeping on board the steamer (I stuck to my salvage night and day) I wasn't disturbed. There was an old hippo that had the bad

low medical plan deflects policy, subconsciousness causes
hysterias. Id's insipid? Try vomit. Hot torrid dyed blonde?
False ideals distorted wants: women's election. Civics' New
Left yawns, sisters irk to swap control. Limits undaunted.
Nether traces of phlegm, brown spatter's gross—traces—
bile submersed spit! Constrictor noose, livid accessory,
reddened neck adaptation scarred from ordeal fright.
Cynics bankrolled anew a trove of debt. Who would kill
for profiting bigots or the chuckle of whooping clowns?
Ensnare rodent scum whippet newly crowned, Senate
despondent. Rehab mates had fueled coup; start cutting new
fashion hem width. Accessory chic a metaphor, a wronged
widow, leather-drag composure and snarling damned
exultation for betrothed. Tanned pectoral lines oblique, the
host Catalan flaming dismayed moods—nasty, crazed,
a sicko chap paid good uppers boldly to hook addict, hearts,
speeds' snafu encounter, bennies to snort; encountered
rotted rotten gland disease. Anglo limits, precarious
booed debacle, applause halted, roulette sapped Dream
folk the vote.

His off-key humming monumental row bugs my manly
Biden's impulsive platitudes, trust has exacerbated his
redraft, Joe begrudged reactionary through reform; sleazy
beard preacher's fraud potential, vets disown Afghanistan.
I dread Likud's pre-fatwa intel; boycott unfounded wars?
An urban colony's pernicious—land critics stir austerely
risk averse. Haunted: chilly baloney moan skit. Wow,
beggars scent poo the most, deadly reek. I severely tried,
eyes-tight constipation. Try implanted digits. They cause
affray—foreign resettlement plan. Deranged with anger;
reclaim manifold land stubbornly, peace plan to hawk,
a bout of zero-consciousness; sundered settler-leaning
Accord for neither (a schmuck who'll cry vantage right away),
insurgence reverbed. Terror's untold widows thereafter Black

habit of getting out on the bank and roaming at night over the station grounds. The pilgrims used to turn out in a body and empty every rifle they could lay hands on at him. Some even had sat up o' nights for him. All this energy was wasted, though. 'That animal has a charmed life,' he said; 'but you can say this only of brutes in this country. No man—you apprehend me?—no man here bears a charmed life.' He stood there for a moment in the moonlight with his delicate hooked nose set a little askew, and his mica eyes glittering without a wink, then, with a curt Good-night, he strode off. I could see he was disturbed and considerably puzzled, which made me feel more hopeful than I had been for days. It was a great comfort to turn from that chap to my influential friend, the battered, twisted, ruined, tin-pot steamboat. I clambered on board. She rang under my feet like an empty Huntley & Palmer biscuit-tin kicked along a gutter; she was nothing so solid in make, and rather less pretty in shape, but I had expended enough hard work on her to make me love her. No influential friend would have served me better. She had given me a chance to come out a bit—to find out what I could do. No, I don't like work. I had rather laze about and think of all the fine things that can be done. I don't like work—no man does—but I like what is in the work—the chance to find yourself. Your own reality—for yourself, not for others—what no other man can ever know. They can only see the mere show, and never can tell what it really means.

"I was not surprised to see somebody sitting aft, on the deck, with his legs dangling over the mud. You see I rather chummed with the few mechanics there were in that station, whom the other pilgrims naturally despised—on account of their imperfect manners, I suppose.

Sabbath, offsetting scout bomber, tanks exploding in light
of devastation sounds. A building's fueled to burn: doubt
hinders rocky land, deadly treachery rivals may feud, break
plans on a whim. Unbeaten expanded concise warning.
Folly's treachery prostrated low. Fanaticals master
armed strife instead; South Sudan sadist's trophy if suits
win corruptly. Golan supplementary?—Jordan fear
dares an armed strife. Likud scares more opponents in
platoon fight, Mid-East delegate brooked woes, bet
a fickle *adieu*, and seized China spies. Twittering
willpower shrinks bandwidth, a dirt feud fight restored
force. Unruly recalls deterred hands deliberately muzzled,
rich trade appeal stores' global stand-by handling malaise.
Lymph nodes' prostate pervert, tube worm of backed crap,
bullseye excremental end, a backward fisted, putrid,
slipshod reamed stoat. Guy pampered m'Lord. Defang
hunger by meat strike assembly, monthly banned martyrs'
prison wing picked a foster Mother; reversed stunning
moronic mistake, a motherless sweetie inmate, cuck bi, dad-
befriended a tough guard clerk, bomber to daily succor.
Coincidental trend skewed Strasbourg's defender.
Jihad infantry finance income's counterfeit—confined
southward by Urdu. Show my stoned dyke twerk. My grand-
mother hazed a scout, then drinks offal, sublime dingbat's
campy fun. I boned file clerk for grandma's butt—alike
bodies finger jerk—advanced, declined poor health. Forlorn
calamity—core poor health, cock sore lover's hot slow
bugger can man-pleasure sow. Hey man, boldly free the
weirdo, endeavored chandelles sought in whisky dreams.

Cyborgs compromised beauty, subtly ridding past of
inequities, expanding owner demand. Sunni
attacker shunned hitherto fanatics; settler annex-
ation dooms the mother victims nationally deprived—
honor bound to bear insurrect banners, PLO's.

This was the foreman—a boiler-maker by trade—a good worker. He was a lank, bony, yellow-faced man, with big intense eyes. His aspect was worried, and his head was as bald as the palm of my hand; but his hair in falling seemed to have stuck to his chin, and had prospered in the new locality, for his beard hung down to his waist. He was a widower with six young children (he had left them in charge of a sister of his to come out there), and the passion of his life was pigeon-flying. He was an enthusiast and a connoisseur. He would rave about pigeons. After work hours he used sometimes to come over from his hut for a talk about his children and his pigeons; at work, when he had to crawl in the mud under the bottom of the steamboat, he would tie up that beard of his in a kind of white serviette he brought for the purpose. It had loops to go over his ears. In the evening he could be seen squatted on the bank rinsing that wrapper in the creek with great care, then spreading it solemnly on a bush to dry.

"I slapped him on the back and shouted, 'We shall have rivets!' He scrambled to his feet exclaiming, 'No! Rivets!' as though he couldn't believe his ears. Then in a low voice, 'You … eh?' I don't know why we behaved like lunatics. I put my finger to the side of my nose and nodded mysteriously. 'Good for you!' he cried, snapped his fingers above his head, lifting one foot. I tried a jig. We capered on the iron deck. A frightful clatter came out of that hulk, and the virgin forest on the other bank of the creek sent it back in a thundering roll upon the sleeping station. It must have made some of the pilgrims sit up in their hovels. A dark figure obscured the lighted doorway of the manager's hut, vanished, then, a second or so after, the doorway itself

Imposter's poor plan, an oil dictator afraid eludes
Berbers. Defaulter bank crony's escrow-based scam wields
picket fence lies. Bid's assets were buried, banned
instead clause appalled at imams' no-fly ban; such despair's
appalling, weaned through snack truck nutrition, stand bad
postured with askew morality, jaundice smeared tongue,
brown mucus taste. Improper misnomer wish scripts
unwritten (V transgressed, then recharged for a Mr. or Ms.;
fusion flouts pairs). Grand attraction: novice wife paused
chicken-frying. Precaution: excuse me, fashion's a
goner, surly mood craves aroused legions. At the Turk
showers V cruised frontlines for Jehovah, promised
drugstore support to spout religions' definitions; network
trends Riyadh forestalled with Assad, plunder begotten
for regime vote, Likud eyed muskrat-smeared prophet's
silver-lined foresight, wordy levy wrought on the wordless.
Steel-capped troops for foreclosure arrears. Drinker,
scheming renewed between thwarted from the ranks, slip-
ping bad stammers, binger geek, dick-bait hair,
embedding shit wantonly: Walker Bush, new guy.

I strapped him on a rack, astounded, "*Inshallah*, limits!"
Recanted through defeat, complaining, "Whoa, limits!"
as doughy puddings relieve piss tears. Men with a bro noise,
"U … A!" Time won't grow timely; depraved wild humor:
pigs fly, pool guy swinger's lunar bride, tough guy bros band
frotted deliriously. "Dude tattoo!" defiled whacked free
thinkers a bloody red, fisting some brute. Aye-ayed the pig.
V labored long, a crying wreck. Delightful scatterbrain gout
of fat bulk, grand subversion promised honor, Samarkand's
hotter, bleak, fetid fracking, a blustering solar dawn, a
weeping nation. Distrust charade, dumb pollster visions split
Rump with hair Donalds. The shark dealer endured
delighted foreplay, monster Kavanaugh's butt ravished,
smelled unpleasant, no more laughter, and toupée with pelt

vanished, too. We stopped, and the silence driven away by the stamping of our feet flowed back again from the recesses of the land. The great wall of vegetation, an exuberant and entangled mass of trunks, branches, leaves, boughs, festoons, motionless in the moonlight, was like a rioting invasion of soundless life, a rolling wave of plants, piled up, crested, ready to topple over the creek, to sweep every little man of us out of his little existence. And it moved not. A deadened burst of mighty splashes and snorts reached us from afar, as though an icthyosaurus had been taking a bath of glitter in the great river. 'After all,' said the boiler-maker in a reasonable tone, 'why shouldn't we get the rivets?' Why not, indeed! I did not know of any reason why we shouldn't. 'They'll come in three weeks,' I said confidently.

"But they didn't. Instead of rivets there came an invasion, an infliction, a visitation. It came in sections during the next three weeks, each section headed by a donkey carrying a white man in new clothes and tan shoes, bowing from that elevation right and left to the impressed pilgrims. A quarrelsome band of footsore sulky niggers trod on the heels of the donkey; a lot of tents, camp-stools, tin boxes, white cases, brown bales would be shot down in the courtyard, and the air of mystery would deepen a little over the muddle of the station. Five such instalments came, with their absurd air of disorderly flight with the loot of innumerable outfit shops and provision stores, that, one would think, they were lugging, after a raid, into the wilderness for equitable division. It was an inextricable mess of things decent in themselves but that human folly made look like the spoils of thieving.

vanquished glue. Key dropped, renters' high rents risen
astray, higher, banking on elite mode's rack of pain
conquered weaknesses (Faulkner's bland). Debate goal:
assimilation; Ceausescu's errant hand embrangled mess
of drunks, paunches, thieves, cows, baboons, hopelessness
in balloon flight, angina dieting vacation for gown-less
wife, a clothing grave for aunts, styled cup-breasted, belly
colossal lowers her cheeks; newspeak Treasury's evil plan's
bogus; rout promised civil resistance. Panic proved what?
The threatened worst, almighty crashes as court's preachers
bomb Dakar, although a rich hero saw us ranting, shaking
a wrath emitter's triggered hate fever. "Alcohol tremor,"
spoiler traitor stringers treasonable zone, spy movements
regret their limits. Try stopping greed! Crisis wrought,
Machiavellian timely movement. Welcome Wiki-
leaks, widespread, profitably.

Buttigiegn't, inbred old bigots share blame; a Caucasian
man: affliction or inspiration? He claimed elections brew in
Midwest elites, East Texan senate hires honky Aryan,
the Right's fans with spewed prose scanned bad news,
howling of annihilation; "fight the rest," boo the repressed
schisms. Immoral command dispute, four grumpy figures
awed from appeals of appointee; uncommon-sense rank
fools, skin-conscious, quite racist; town jail's rookie caught
clowning, escort guard panders heir of history who'd
treason a whistleblower for struggle for narration. Thrive
much in torments? Shame, despair incurred share of
deformity, smite trigger boot of maneuverable mounted
cops, end precision wars, rat run could sync laser
bugging, pastor's crusade issues a scripture-less, disreputable
revision. Inconstantly equitable press of limbs augmenting
stem cells; butt-crack Cuban naughty phrasebook:
wild gargoyles excreting.

"This devoted band called itself the Eldorado Exploring Expedition, and I believe they were sworn to secrecy. Their talk, however, was the talk of sordid buccaneers: it was reckless without hardihood, greedy without audacity, and cruel without courage; there was not an atom of foresight or of serious intention in the whole batch of them, and they did not seem aware these things are wanted for the work of the world. To tear treasure out of the bowels of the land was their desire, with no more moral purpose at the back of it than there is in burglars breaking into a safe. Who paid the expenses of the noble enterprise I don't know; but the uncle of our manager was leader of that lot.

"In exterior he resembled a butcher in a poor neighbourhood, and his eyes had a look of sleepy cunning. He carried his fat paunch with ostentation on his short legs, and during the time his gang infested the station spoke to no one but his nephew. You could see these two roaming about all day long with their heads close together in an everlasting confab.

"I had given up worrying myself about the rivets. One's capacity for that kind of folly is more limited than you would suppose. I said Hang!—and let things slide. I had plenty of time for meditation, and now and then I would give some thought to Kurtz. I wasn't very interested in him. No. Still, I was curious to see whether this man, who had come out equipped with moral ideas of some sort, would climb to the top after all and how he would set about his work when there."

Lease-promoted bank sprawled in wealth resells gestapo's extorting acquisitions, slammed by bereaved, favors born too greedily. Deadlock of terror fosters flock of morbid puppeteers: deplores feckless in cloud Hollywood, seedy about voracity, strapped mule in ploughed carriage; rebels sought Sam Adams or Coors Light for oblivious deception with a soul patch amendment, jaded mock dream to share; stealings accounted corner perks undeserved. New rare pleasure: mouth alters vowels; saucer lands, Roswell's entire gizmo's core floral circus, dabblers' sack of shit; end rendition murders taking it to the grave. New trade for defenses for the global westernized. Cyclone blow, hunger struggle or dour massacre cause fever for jackpots.

An inferior treaty leveled Fallujah's inter-war traitor feud, Yankee's lies fed a crook on greedy money. His rape deed fits Assange with allegation of his court dregs, enduring the crime shebang, arrested, the nation woke to slogans from his refuge. Shoo Qaddafi's coup, stoning devout, shawl-grey throng wield prayers' death throes forever in a tremor, grasping Conrad.

By attrition, blood money ring buys wealth bailout for credits. Guns' fatality combats mind or body in war, WikiLeaked men who could disclose. Why harangue the trembling tide? Try assembly, the prime of agitation, end how tanned men die, you'd grieve, gunshots or worse. Avoidant, wary, infested within. So chill, Marco's Rubio's snoopy where Kyrgyzstan's crew have gunpowder crypt; we'd quarrel Crimea's lost support, good time to talk shop at the Mall and vow renewed pressures' clout reverse healthcare.

AfterWords: Ghost Stories

V, as they're known to their friends, realizes their true self, less as a process of coming out and more one of coming together: a multiple self as a complexly accumulated meshing of histories, experiences, and imaginings. V's story consists of the mental chatter, the unspoken and unspeakable desires, avarice, anxieties, and political resentments of guests at a wedding party on a cruise ship that's quarantined and adrift. While heavily anchored in an ongoing present, the writing is also formally adrift, flitting across psycho-socialities, in a manner similar to psychoanalysis but with no trajectory towards a cure, pulled instead through multiple intersections by (pre)dominantly human—lunatic rather than lunar—tides.

The autobiography of V lives within, between, and against another text: Joseph Conrad's *Heart of Darkness* (1899)—a text that continues to assign bodies by race and racialized gender. In its assignation of how someone like V can be in the world, that work (*Darkness*) is unavoidable despite damnations by scholars such as Chinua Achebe, who considered it irredeemable while acknowledging Conrad as "one of the great stylists of modern fiction"—precisely what makes him so widely read (and so insidious).[1] Achebe identified Conrad as a "bloody racist," whose racism is so normative that "its manifestations go completely undetected."[2] I agree, but for the same reasons remain hesitant to dismiss Conrad. It's not that I seek to redeem his work, but to point to its continuing effect within that world where we (and V) can be told in myriad ways to go back where and when we came from (I take this to mean less to a geographical location and more to a social position, our "proper" place).

Ark of Martyrs is a sound work (and an unsound one) that readers are required to translate and sound out for themselves. It's derived from the school method of dictation in language classes whereby the teacher reads aloud a text and the students write it down. What might appear as physical, linguistic, social, or cultural mishearing or mistranslating, are instead activated into forms of dissent so that the otherwise disciplinary processes of racialization and gendering can be enacted as highly mobile, resistant, perhaps *chosen* conditions even as they are assigned fixity.

The core of *Darkness*—which pervades its every description—is the encounter between white and black. At one side is the idealized "Intended," the virginal fiancée waiting in Europe whose (white) face bears and bares the "delicate shade of truthfulness," though the façade of that "truth" depends on separation (perhaps segregation) from its inverse, the famously doubled "horror" of sexualized blackness, whether of impenetrable "jungle," of depthless waters, or of cannibalistic male bodies and bestial female bodies. *Martyrs*, while parallel in dysphoric carnality, and rather than the febrile blackness that terrorizes *Darkness*, is instead indebted to the Black multivocalities of Creole, Santeria, gospel, toasting, and rap.

Another reference for this rewriting—though I may be out on an art historical limb here—is Kazimir Malevich's 1915 painting, *Black Square*, which marks the seemingly non-racial, but ideologically based birth of Suprematism, and marks a pivotal moment for the development of

European modernism. The 2015 discovery that Malevich's canvas, under its top coat of black paint, contains a racial inscription, "Battle of negroes in a dark cave" makes it even more overtly, and subtextually, a foundational moment for modernism. *Black Square*, or *BS* (if I may), has been variously discussed as the death of painting and as the birth of a revolutionary new art. In blackface, *BS* is a bastion of white supremacism. We might see it as a racialized haunting of broader art histories, similar to how blackness was a perennial antithesis of Conrad's notion of civilization.

In "light" of Conrad's colonialist configuration of time, I take the *liberté* to propose that *Ark of Martyrs* prefigures his, that *Martyrs* is the undertext of *Darkness*—the clean dirt of the world, the dissent of an assigned body, the brown space between, the underwriting before the whitewash—that mine is the joke (*avant la lettre*, pardon my French) beneath his racist, misogynist, xenophobic exterior.

—Allan deSouza

1 Chinua Achebe, *An Image of Africa: Racism in Conrad's 'Heart of Darkness,'* Massachusetts Review. 18. 1977.

2 Chinua Achebe, "Commentary," *Heart of Darkness & Selections from The Congo Diary*, Modern Library, NY, 1999. xlix.

Acknowledgements

Thanks: #VivianSming; #Yaddo

About the Author

Allan deSouza is a California-based trans-media artist whose works restage colonial-era material legacies through counter-strategies of humor, fabulation, and (mis)translation.

deSouza's work has been shown extensively in the US and internationally, including at the Krannert Museum, IL; the Phillips Collection, Washington, D.C.; and the Pompidou Centre, Paris. deSouza's book, *How Art Can Be Thought* (Duke, 2018), examines art pedagogy, and proposes decolonizing artistic, viewing, and pedagogical practices that can form new attachments within the contemporary world. The book provides an extensive analytical glossary of some of the most common terms used to discuss art, while considering how those terms may be adapted to new artistic and social challenges. deSouza is represented by Talwar Gallery, NY and New Delhi, and is Chair of the Department of Art Practice at University of California, Berkeley.

Ark of Martyrs: An Autobiography of V

Allan deSouza

Heart of Darkness: Part I

Joseph Conrad
Excerpt from *Heart of Darkness & Selections from The Congo Diary*
(New York: Modern Library Paperback Edition), 1999

Cover photo by

Allan deSouza

Design by

Sming Sming Books

Published by

Sming Sming Books (Saratoga, CA)
Wolfman Books (410 13th St. Oakland, CA 94612)

Distributed by

Small Press Distribution

ISBN 978-0-9985006-8-3

Sming Sming Books + **WOLFMAN**